YOU
FOUND
ME

ALSO BY MICHELLE DYKMAN

Her Sanctuary, His Heart

If Only In My Dreams
A SNOWY SPRINGS ROMANCE | BOOK ONE

The Deal with Dakota
A SNOWY SPRINGS ROMANCE | BOOK TWO

You, Me, and the Stars
BETHEL PRIVATE SCHOOL SERIES | BOOK ONE

Someone Like You
BETHEL PRIVATE SCHOOL SERIES | BOOK TWO

MICHELLE DYKMAN

BETHEL PRIVATE SCHOOL SERIES | BOOK THREE

Ambassador International
GREENVILLE, SOUTH CAROLINA & BELFAST, NORTHERN IRELAND

www.ambassador-international.com

YOU FOUND ME

©2023 by Michelle Dykman
All rights reserved

Hardcover ISBN: 978-1-64960-439-2
Paperback ISBN: 978-1-64960-400-2
eISBN: 978-1-64960-394-4
Library of Congress Control Number: 2023935847

Cover design by Hannah Linder Designs
Interior Typesetting by Dentelle Design
Digital Edition by Anna Riebe Raats
Edited by Katie Cruice Smith and Macy Johnson

Scripture taken from the Holy Bible, New International Version®, NIV® Copyright ©1973, 1978, 1984, 2011 by Biblica, Inc.® Used by permission. All rights reserved worldwide.

AMBASSADOR INTERNATIONAL
Emerald House House Group, Inc.
411 University Ridge, Suite B14
Greenville, SC 29601, USA
www.ambassador-international.com

AMBASSADOR BOOKS
The Mount
2 Woodstock Link
Belfast, BT6 8DD, Northern Ireland, UK
www.ambassadormedia.co.uk

The colophon is a trademark of Ambassador, a Christian publishing company.

DEDICATION

When the world seems dark, there is always hope.

To those who fight the battle everyday: you are my heroes. I hope this story does your struggle justice.

"When my spirit grows faint within me,
it is you who watch over my way."
—Psalm 142:3a

AUTHOR'S NOTE

Suicide, depression, and mental illness are words that have become synonymous with today's society. There are countless people from all walks of life who face the daily challenges of living with these. Being a high school teacher has brought me face to face with the realities and pressures working to overpower the love of God for many of the young people with whom I spend my days. In writing this book, my desire is that the message of hope and grace that is so freely bestowed on us by Christ's sacrifice reaches from these pages to the heart of all who read it.

CHAPTER ONE

A *hangover is not a bad way to die.* At least, the pounding in her head was trying to convince her of this fact. Amy Carter reached blindly to stop the incessant chiming of her phone alarm. Her mouth tasted like yesterday's garbage. *Ugh.* Too bad drinking herself to stupidity didn't have the desired effect. She was still here. *Unlike Olivia.*

She swallowed hard pushing back the memories of her cousin and closest friend. Olivia wouldn't have been stupid enough to down bottle after bottle until she passed out. She had been strong. Stronger than Amy.

Sighing, she rushed her hands through the tangled threads of black hair covering her face, pressing it back from her eyes and marshaling her reluctance under control to start the day.

"Amy, it's time for school," her mother said, peeking her head into Amy's doorway and then out again.

Thankfully, she didn't come into the room like she did on most days, or Amy really would have been in trouble. The after-effects of last nights binge were evidenced all over her make-up smudged face.

Showering and finding a cute outfit took longer than she'd have liked, due to the construction crew pounding out a rhythm behind her eye sockets. Pity she'd never developed that sultry shape Olivia had always joked she would. Settling her tank top over her high-waisted ripped jeans, she inhaled the zipper closed, glancing at the time on her phone and groaning. If she didn't have her tail downstairs in the next two minutes, her mother would come looking for her.

Dirty clothes safely stashed at the bottom of the laundry basket, she applied one last swipe of eyeliner and rushed out of the room.

"Amy, what in the world?" Her mother's eyes went wide, as they did most mornings when she saw Amy's choice of clothes. "Amy Carter, if you think . . . " And here it came.

"What?" Amy asked, glancing down at her outfit. Everything was covered, so what was her mother's problem?

Fay Carter looked like her daughter: green eyes, hair as black as pitch, and an apple-shaped body. Amy's mother's shape was more mature than hers, naturally, but it wasn't difficult to see where Amy got her looks. Apples were apples, and they didn't fall far from the tree—at least when it came to body shape.

"That," her mother said, gesturing to her daughter's outfit, "is inappropriate for school. Go and change." She paused and studied Amy. "Did you get any sleep last night?"

"Why? I happen to like what I'm wearing. And yes, a full eight hours." Lies, all of it—but better for her mother than reality. The truth was that the impromptu party in the park—courtesy of Felicia—hadn't broken up till four a.m—not that she would ever tell her mother that. She'd be so dead.

"What you are wearing is more suited for a party than school, and I know the administration would say the same." Her mother's voice hardened. "Now, please go upstairs and put on something more suitable."

With another roll of her eyes and a loud huff, Amy stormed back to her room, ripping off her clothes as she went. She glanced at the time, bit her lip, and quickly slipped into a fashionable pair of light skinny jeans and a purple butterfly-sleeve peplum top that just met the waistband of her jeans, all the while wishing her mother was more like Felicia's or Willow's mothers. Nothing Felicia or Willow did seemed to bother them. Instead, her mother complained about everything. Her clothes, her grades, her hair.

Instantly, she felt bad. Her mother loved her; Amy knew she did. But was it too much to ask for her to be happy with something Amy did, just for once?

She glanced at the outfit she'd just taken off and impulsively shoved it into her backpack. She'd change at school. What her mother didn't know wouldn't hurt her.

A honk sounded from outside. Felicia was here. Zipping her backpack closed, she scanned her messy room, hoping she'd remembered everything she'd need before booking it back to the kitchen.

Amy's mother was still scurrying around, preparing breakfast and packing lunches. Her father would be down soon, computer in one hand and phone in the other. Both of her parents worked long hours; some nights, it was just her at home now that her brother, Logan, was in college. She was alone, the walls pressing down on her, chanting the tune that spelled out her grief. Some nights, it seemed that it would be better if the accident had taken her instead of Olivia. She was the one who had deserved to live, not Amy.

Forcing down the dry cereal with some orange juice, she ran for the front door. "Bye, Mom."

"Bye. Be sure to—"

The door closed behind Amy, cutting off anything else her mother might have said.

"Hey, girl! Lovely morning, isn't it?" Felicia asked with a grin.

"Yeah, about as lovely as not getting to choose my own outfit," Amy muttered as she flung her school bag into the backseat before sliding into the passenger seat of the car and clicking in her seatbelt.

Felicia raised an eyebrow. "Are you okay?"

Amy shrugged, her anger from earlier quickly fading. "What? Yeah. Fine." Felicia was a good friend, but they weren't BFFs—not like she and Olivia had been. Olivia was the only one who knew all about Amy's depression and helped carry her secrets. Swallowing hard against the lump in her throat, Amy blinked rapidly, glancing at her friend.

Felicia shrugged, leaned back into her seat, and slid the gearshift to drive, her light brown afro bobbing in time with her movements. Felicia was stunning. Her big, blue eyes contrasted with her softly toned, brown skin. She had the kind of figure any girl their age would crave; add to it Felicia's knack for style and outgoing personality, and it was no wonder that she was so popular. Amy often wondered why Felicia still hung out with her.

Swallowing back a wave of self-pity, Amy slipped her phone from her pocket and began scrolling through her social media feed. Her stomach clenched painfully as images raced past her eyes.

"Hey, did you hear that Haley Bieber got a modeling gig with Gucci?" Felicia asked, handing her phone to Amy. Amy glanced at the stunning woman dressed in mile-high gold stiletto heels, her thin body seductively sheathed in a floor-length, gold dress. Long, blonde hair flowed like a wave of sunshine over her back, and her lips tilted in an ecstatic smile. Amy would never look like this girl. Apples didn't look good in gold.

"Wow, she's stunning. And look at those legs . . . " Amy handed the phone back to Felicia, trying without success to erase the images from her mind. Like a technicolor film, the glaring differences between Amy's figure and the girl in the picture played in her mind.

"I know, right?" Felicia dropped the phone into a cup holder and turned down the street, heading for Bethel Private School. A few minutes later, the car came to a stop in the parking lot.

Amy tried to mimic the graceful way Felicia moved as she climbed out of the car. She didn't succeed. Brad Thorn, Jace Antilles, and a few other boys from their usual group waited outside the school entrance. Since Willow's unfortunate accident, everyone seemed unsettled, like worker bees unsure of what to do without their queen.

Brad seemed to take it the worst. Black circles underlined his deep blue eyes, and fatigue hung on his frame. Amy didn't have the courage to ask him about it, although anyone with eyes could see that he was struggling. She hurt for him—and for Felicia. Both of their lives had changed since the event. There was no sympathy in her for Willow, though; she deserved whatever she got.

"Are you going to visit Willow sometime?" Willow had been in a serious car accident a month back and was still in a coma. No one knew when she would wake up.

Felicia stiffened. "Nah, I don't want to see her."

Willow and Felicia had a complicated history. They didn't like to talk about it, but there was a rumor going around that Willow had stolen Felicia's first love. It wouldn't surprise Amy. Willow was that kind of person. She'd thought of asking Felicia about it, but seeing the way Felicia's face would pinch into an expression of pain if someone mentioned it, Amy just didn't have the heart. If Felicia wanted to share that with Amy, she would.

Pushing her way through the surge of bodies, Amy reached her locker and put in the combination before pulling out books for her first class.

"Hey, Amy," Brad said. His locker was beside hers, so they often ran into one another there.

"Hey." She blinked, again noticing the dark lines under his eyes. "Are you okay?"

Brad shrugged, tugging his hand through his hair. "Yeah, fine."

He looked anything but fine, and she hoped the smell of alcohol wasn't as noticeable to everyone else as it was to her. Maybe she should say something.

"You might want to pop some gum or something."

Brad's frown deepened. "Yeah, thanks." He exhaled heavily and squeezed his eyelids closed before opening them again. She'd heard about Brad's old girlfriend, Candice Hillman, being pregnant and her disappearance from school. Everyone had. Was that what was bothering him? Why would it, though? Wasn't he with Willow? She couldn't bring herself to ask. Secrets, after all, were secrets; and she had plenty of them. Brad could keep his to himself.

The warning bell pealed down the hallway. Amy thrust her backpack into a space in her locker, checking her books again before slamming it shut. Brad did the same, at a much slower pace. Ignoring the urge to hurry him along, she ran to her first class, lest Mrs. Wilson ream her out for being tardy or absent again.

She'd unintentionally missed so many classes in the last few months. Mornings were not good for her, even on the nights she didn't sneak out. At times, it took all the strength she had to lift herself from bed and begin another day. The feeling had worsened since Olivia's passing, her grief taking what was left of it. The bell rang, and she made it to her seat just in time.

"How are you feeling after last night?" Felicia asked.

"Man, this hangover is going to be the death of me," she said dramatically, gesturing to her head.

Felicia laughed and slipped into her seat as Mrs. Wilson brought the class to order and began handing out the previous day's assignments. Brad glanced at Willow's empty seat, his expression ambivalent.

What was he looking for?

"Amy Carter?" Mrs. Wilson said, beckoning her to the front of the room. Amy rose from her seat and walked to where Mrs. Wilson stood behind her desk. Her stomach clenched tighter, and she felt the acid from her orange juice creep up her throat.

"Yes?"

"Amy, I would like to discuss your final assignment. There seems to be some confusion about what was required."

What?

Mrs. Wilson swung the papers around and laid them on her desk. A pang of shock reverberated through Amy as she saw the grade. In bold red, the letter F was encircled beside her name. Ten percent of her final grade and she got an F. How? She'd spent all of last Saturday on the assignment.

"I don't understand."

Mrs. Wilson's expression softened. "Amy, I explained the assignment clearly when it was given to you. We had numerous discussions regarding the importance of this project, and I do believe you were given ample opportunity to ask for clarification."

How had she gotten an F? Amy swallowed hard, fighting back the tears clogging her throat.

Mrs. Wilson let out a deep breath. "Amy, I know you have some struggles with this course, but this can't continue. You will spend the next three lunch periods redoing this assignment if you want to pass. I will remind you that this is ten percent of your final grade."

Blindly taking the paper Mrs. Wilson handed her, she shuffled back to her seat. The heavy beat of her heart gave her notice of what would come next, and she knew the feeling of the attack all too well. It often came in her nightmares where her secrets haunted her. Tingles skittered through her fingertips as her blood raced through her veins. The air became thick—almost too heavy to breathe. She had to leave, had to get out of the class before she embarrassed herself completely. Nausea followed the tingles. She grasped the edge of the desk shakily.

"May I go to the bathroom?" Amy asked, almost whispering.

All she needed was a nod, and Amy was out of the room, as if the hounds of Hades were behind her.

CHAPTER TWO

"Amy? Amy, are you in here?" The bathroom door squeaked as Felicia entered the room.

Amy lifted her feet and hugged her knees closer as she sat atop the closed toilet. The silver walls around her dulled her reflection in the fluorescent light. Anger, shame, and embarrassment flooded her body with warmth that was entirely unpleasant. The panic attack had passed the moment she'd thrown up, although the side effects still lingered—tingles in her hands and numbness in her lips. She tested her lips again with her tongue but remained silent. The only person she'd ever told of her panic attacks was Olivia, and that secret had died with her. Grief gripped her throat. She swallowed hard, struggling to contain her roiling emotions.

The heavy door squeaked open and then clicked closed again, signaling Felicia's exit. Amy released a heavy breath and held a second one, waiting for any sign of life. All was quiet. Amy climbed off the toilet and swung the cubicle door open. The room was empty. Moving to the sink, she splashed cold water on her face, cooling her heated cheeks. She looked up. Reflected back at her were tired, bloodshot eyes and a round face that was pale and too full surrounded by messy, dark strands plastered to it with sweat. *Ugly*, she thought. The mild ache in her skull from this morning had transformed into a raging headache. Why couldn't she do anything right? Why couldn't she be good enough?

With an unsteady hand, she gently cleaned the dark lines of mascara running from her eyes and down her cheeks. If only her memories could be washed away as easily.

Arranging her features into stillness devoid of emotion, she straightened her spine, threw back her shoulders, and plastered on a fake smile. She tugged her blouse straight and mushed her hair up into a messy bun atop her head, sighing again at her soft middle.

If only she had inherited more of her father's genes than her mother's, she'd be lanky like him, rather than round like her aunts. Maybe then she'd be satisfied with how she looked. The boys would want her like they wanted Felicia and Willow. Maybe then she would feel like more than just a placeholder. Maybe she would believe she was more than just a willing body and an easy fix. She swallowed down a wave of disgust at herself and stared hard into the mirror until her image blurred before her eyes. No, she wouldn't cry.

The warning bell for the next period pierced the silence and was soon joined by the bustle of students. Amy quickly wiped the remaining water from her hands and face and hurried to the science lab to retrieve her bag, but it was gone. Oh, well. She would figure that out later. She had Nutrition and Health class next, and she couldn't afford to be late. Hopefully, they were baking today, and she wouldn't need her books.

She entered the class only to be stopped by an arm in a letterman jacket. The hand held her backpack.

"Wilson insisted I bring this for you," Brad said.

"Oh, thanks."

He shrugged and dropped the bag at her feet. They both glanced down at it. "Sorry," he mumbled and took his place at his station.

Sighing, she lifted the bag from the floor. "No problem." He didn't acknowledge her. Maybe he didn't hear her. Whatever. The class was about to start.

The disaster in science compounded what was turning out to be a catastrophe of a day. First, she forgot to add eggs; then the oven was set too high, burning her Bundt cake to a dark crisp. That wouldn't have been the worst thing to happen, except the smoke from the burned pastry set off the fire alarm, forcing the entire school out onto the football field. Cheeks hot, Amy ducked her head, unable to meet Mrs. Schoeman's furious gaze from the front of the line. No doubt she would fail the lesson.

Her stomach quivered with unease. She drew a few more deep breaths. Her hands shook as she covered her eyes, swallowing hard. She wouldn't cry. Dying of embarrassment was not a bad way to go. After ten minutes and a whispered conversation between Principal Rory and Mrs. Schoeman, they were allowed to return to class.

"You okay?" Brad asked as they walked back to class. He didn't laugh at her; his expression seemed to be one of concern rather than amusement.

"Yes. I just can't believe I did that."

Brad shrugged. "At least, you weren't the only one. And it's warm today," he added.

It was true. Nancy Cauldwell's cake was as black as hers, but no one seemed to be staring at Nancy the way they were at Amy. The smell of fresh flowers, cut grass, and warm air caught her nose. If she wasn't so mortified, she might have enjoyed the smell.

"I guess."

Brad squeezed her shoulder gently before returning to his station. Under the watchful eye of Mrs. Schoeman, Amy quickly remade her cake, careful to follow the recipe to the letter. This one turned out much better than the last, and with a lighter heart, she left for lunch.

The remainder of the school day flew by, thankfully without further disasters if she overlooked the glances and whispers from the girl's volleyball team. A glare and raised eyebrow from Felicia quickly shut them up.

Felicia drove her home from school, but she steered the conversation away from any of the day's disasters and focused on shallower subjects instead.

"Thanks. I'll see you tomorrow," Amy said, waving as Felicia pulled out of the driveway. She ran up the porch steps of the two-story bungalow. Her house wasn't nearly as nice as Candice's or Willow's—she was embarrassed to invite her friends home. But it was her safe place. The familiar, dark gray building with the garage on the left and wide bay windows on the right was her home. Her bedroom window, which had a view over the main street, sat above the front door, allowing her easy access to the roof and garden for her forays with her friends at night.

Her mother's white Honda SUV and her father's blue Toyota sedan were parked in front of closed garage doors. That was unusual. A sudden dread gripped her stomach. Why were both of her parents home at this time of the day? Had something happened? Her mother sometimes came home from her job as a designer at a marketing company around the same time as Amy, but her father was rarely home before the sun sank below the horizon.

The knot in her stomach, undissolved after her panic attack earlier, hardened and grew larger as she pushed open the front door. Her bag slid off her shoulder, falling to the floor beside a light gray sofa. Heated voices exploded from the direction of the kitchen. Unnerved, she pressed her back to the wall and peeked around the corner.

With the kitchen island between them, her parents stared at each other. Tension pulsed in the air around them. Her mother's posture was rigid, her face red. Her father cleared his throat and bowed his head. His pleading outstretched arms falling to his sides. What in the world was going on?

"This is the end, Gerald. I took you back the first time you allowed her into our lives. But fool me once, shame on you; fool me twice . . . " Her mother trailed off, her voice husky with anger and unshed tears. Amy's chest spasmed at the pain in her mother's voice. "I want you out of this house now."

"Fay, please—I promise you, it's over. What you saw today was not what it looked like."

Her mother was at her father's office? She never went there.

Her mother reeled back as if slapped. "What I witnessed today was you and that *tramp* getting real friendly on that sofa. And it sure didn't look like nothing, the way her hand was tangled in your tie and hair."

What? My father? A cheat? Amy stumbled over the edge of the blue and gray striped rug as she backpedaled. No, this couldn't be happening. Her family was normal. Her parents loved each other. Her dad would never do that . . . But he had. The proof was there in her mother's face. As one, her parents turned, their expressions identically dismayed.

"Amy," her mother said as she moved toward her. "What are you doing home so early?" Her mother's gaze swept to the multi-colored clock, which hung above the dinner table. Her eyes widened, and then her expression smoothed into one of concern, with a hint of embarrassment. "I guess the time got away from us." Her father grumbled something and shifted from one foot to the other.

"Amy, what you heard . . ." her father began.

"Is it true? Dad? Did you cheat on Mom?" Was everything in her life conspiring against her? She couldn't believe this—first Olivia died; then she kept messing up at school, and now *this.*

"Now, baby, it's not what you think."

"Isn't it? Because unless I slipped into another dimension, that's *exactly* what I heard when I walked in here."

A dull red filled her father's cheeks, his expression melting into guilt. *Figures.* "Amy . . ."

She didn't stick around to hear what he would say next. Lifting her backpack from the floor, Amy spun on her heel and launched herself up the stairs to her room, slamming the door for good measure. The backpack crashed into the corner where she flung it, and then the room was still. Exhausted, she stretched out onto her unmade bed and breathed deeply, willing away the tears that were so near the surface.

She lay there for several moments, her heart thundering in her chest, anger hot in her veins. How could her dad do this to her mom? Amy had always thought of her parents as a great couple. They weren't perfect, but they loved each other in their own strange way. The phone rattled in her shaking palm as she tried—without success—to get a hold of Logan; he had to know what he was missing by not being at home. But the call went straight to voicemail.

She checked the time. Four p.m. Logan must be at work. His job at the campus bookstore helped pay his tuition, and he was there most afternoons. Flinging the phone to the far side of her bed, she rolled onto her back and stared at the ceiling. Patterns of constellations, starships, and planets littered the dark blue canvas above her. Her dad put them there when she was six and going through her astronomy phase. Her father was a good man, one who knew how to treat a woman. She snorted. Or so she'd thought.

"Amy," her father said quietly from the other side of her closed door. "Honey, can I come in?"

Amy shook her head, willing herself to remain silent. Her heart ached for her mother, her fury at her father doubling. Who was this other woman? If she hadn't overheard the argument between her father and her mother, she never would have believed something so terrible of him.

"Amy, I love you, and what is going on between your mother and me will never change that."

She suppressed the words wanting to escape from her lips. *Whatever.*

After a long moment, she heard a loud sigh and then the shuffle of footsteps as her father walked away. Grabbing her phone, she swallowed hard against the threatening tears. She opened her messages app, found Felicia's number, and sent a quick *SOS*. Rolling onto her stomach and resting her head on her hands, she waited for a reply. Seconds later, her phone beeped.

On my way, Felicia responded.

Sliding her phone into the back pocket of her pants, Amy opened her bedroom window and climbed out onto the roof tiles. She was careful not to slip as she scurried down the drainpipe and landed, crouched, on the grass below, where she waited for her friend to arrive. Felicia always stopped a few driveways down for her when she snuck out, and today was no exception. The passenger door was open, and Amy slid inside the car.

"What's going on?" Felicia asked, without preamble.

Amy fought back tears as she relayed the story. When she reached the part about her father, Felicia gasped in sympathy, pulling Amy into a quick hug.

"I'm so sorry, Amy. You want to get out of here?"

"Yeah."

Felicia slid the gearshift into drive, and they were gone.

CHAPTER THREE

The bottle was cold in her hand, and small drops of condensation wet her palm. Amy watched droplets fall from the bottle of bright pink liquid and form a wet puddle on the wooden stairs between her jean-covered legs. The sounds of the party surrounded her—loud music with a driving bass, the shuffle of shoes against the laminate flooring, and voices—some filled with laughter, and others that, well, made her blush. The cold wall pressed against her back; her thin, red tank wasn't much protection from it. It was Friday night, and the week had gone from one disaster to the next. She'd failed her math test; her father was gone and the gnawing feeling that this world would be a better place without her played like a song on repeat in her mind.

"Amy, girl, come on," Felicia said, smiling, trying to get her attention. She was plastered against Jace's chest. He pulled her closer and kissed her deeply. Amy turned away—not because she was embarrassed by their amorous display but because it reminded her of the times she'd come into a room to find her parents in a similar embrace.

Lies. It was all lies.

Tipping the bottle up to her lips, she emptied the remaining contents into her mouth and grimaced as the strong alcohol burned her throat. It felt good, unlike the blazing pain in her chest and overwhelming sense of devastation that had haunted her since her cousin's untimely passing. Holding the bottle to a small stretch of light, she giggled at its vacant depths. She needed another one.

Pushing to her feet, she stumbled to the bathroom and tripped over a pair of feet two steps away from the door. The bottle slipped from her hands and crashed to the floor, glass splintering in all directions.

She glanced into the shadows to see Brad passed out in a heap at the top of the wooden staircase beside the bathroom door. He lay on his back, eyes closed, his face creased in a grimace, like whatever he saw behind his eyelids was hurting him. She snorted. What did he know about pain? He had it all—good looks, good grades, and a free ride to college. What was his excuse for drinking himself to stupidity? He hadn't suffered. Not like her, he didn't know the pain of losing someone close to him, didn't know the devastation of the passing of his best friend.

Amy bent to collect the glass, her bare hands scraping the shards. Hands full, she pushed open the bathroom door with her shoulder, groaning as the blinding white light bit into her irises. She dumped the glass into the trash can, fascinated by the small, bloody spots on her hands. The crimson drops mesmerized her. So easy, so simple. Life ran in those small, red droplets. Her life. Oddly, a pain beat where the cuts bled on her hands, each drop taking some of her overwhelming anguish with it. Maybe if she set it free, her pain would stop.

Her fingers closed over the largest shard. The splintered edges cut into the soft skin of her palm, but she barely felt it. One swipe and she wouldn't have to face the world alone anymore. No one would miss her.

Each time she lifted a bottle to her mouth, a part of her hoped it would end her life in some way. An accident. Poisoning. She focused on the red droplets forming pools in her palm. She brought the shard closer to her wrist and pressed it to her skin.

Freedom. Peace. Dizziness crept like curtains closing on the production that was her life. It was the final act, and then the play would end. Drip by drip, the crimson liquid spilled from her veins.

And then, only blackness.

Light pierced the darkness temporarily, pushing back the heavy blanket of shadows that held her under. Murmured voices wove in and out of her consciousness.

"Amy Carter, seventeen, suicide attempt."

That was her name—someone must know where she was. She wanted to ask, but she couldn't seem to open her eyes; and the voices faded again as the darkness dragged her back into its welcoming clutches.

Pain interrupted her peace there, as if someone had grabbed a hold of her and tied her firmly down to something. *Ouch!* Did they know they were hurting her? A glow beckoned her closer to it, promising peace, happiness, and most of all, relief.

"Amy, can you hear me?" a high-pitched, feminine voice coaxed.

No. She wanted to stay in the peace; in leaving, there was pain. The emptiness consumed her again, and she let herself float. Voices and colors filled the void as she soared, weightless, above endless nothing.

"Amy, are you awake?" another alto asked. Gentle hands brushed her forehead, and there was comfort in the touch. The voice became louder, encouraging her, almost like a group of fans cheering her closer. She could hear them speaking, but the fluffy clouds that filled her ears muffled the exact words.

"Is she awake?" That voice she knew; it was broken, husky—but still, she knew it. Amy pressed her eyelids together, hard. If she opened her eyes, the voice would know; she would find out—and there would be only disappointment.

"I'm not sure, Mrs. Carter." The alto spoke again before the void took her once more.

Time seemed to stand still as she floated, neither in the world nor out of it.

"Amy, honey, wake up." *Now* he chose to care. No, she didn't want him here, either. He'd betrayed them. He didn't care about them. She didn't need him, either.

"Mr. and Mrs. Carter, why don't we let her rest. She will wake up when she's ready."

Please listen to her.

The door opened and closed with a soft bang. Amy cracked her eyes open to slits. The room was empty, except for a heap of a human being who sat in a low chair, his body hunched over and his black hair scrunched between his hands. They were almost carbon copies, she and Logan, despite the two-year age gap. Did he know? Why was he here? Logan stirred, and she opened her eyes fully.

"L-Logan," she rasped. Her throat hurt.

Logan's head lifted, his bloodshot eyes meeting hers. "You're awake. Let me get Mom and Dad." He shifted to standing moving for the door, leaving it ajar in his passing.

The sorrow and agony in his voice caused her an echoing pain—proof that she had been right that their lives would be better without her. Pity she could not rid them of herself so easily.

"Oh, Amy." Her mother hurried to her side, her pale hands shaking as she reached to gently curl around Amy's shoulders. She drew Amy into her chest, holding her close. Amy inhaled the familiar smell of her mother's body and swallowed back the barrage of tears clogging her throat. "I'm sorry," she whispered.

"I couldn't—I didn't . . . " Amy cleared her throat. "I needed to stop the pain," she said softly. It seemed so simple, so easy: two cuts and the world as she knew it would be gone. She would be gone.

Her mother eased her back. "Oh, baby, I'm so sorry. I love you." The words felt true; although, as quickly as she believed them, the feeling was stolen away by doubt.

Her father tentatively circled her mother and drew Amy into an embrace. "Please forgive me, I let you down, I promise I won't do it again."

Amy let herself be held. *Just this once,* she thought as she faded into darkness once more.

A ragged breath cracked the din, waking her again. Logan sat in an uncomfortable-looking plastic chair beside her bed. Her parents were nowhere to be seen. Logan lifted his head and smiled, the relief evident in his dark brown eyes.

"Hey," he said softly. "Mom and Dad just stepped out to get some coffee."

She nodded.

A gentle knock sounded on the door. Logan rose from his chair and turned to the door as it opened. A kind-looking doctor and nurse entered the room.

"I'm Dr. Hauser, and this is Nurse Jane. We've come to see how you're doing." Logan didn't move. "Stand aside, son. Nurse Jane needs to check her vitals, blood pressure, and wounds."

Logan reluctantly nodded and stepped aside, watching the doctor warily.

The ties around Amy's wrists slid to the floor. She tried flexing them one at a time to restore blood flow, but her skin was stiff and unyielding. Nurse Jane gently unwrapped more bandages to reveal a jagged cut, running from midway between her wrist and elbow and ending at her pulse. There was a neat row of black stitches underneath the transparent plaster that covered the wound.

Logan's eyes went wide. A small gasp escaped him. Tears glistened in his eyes. His callused hand landed on her shoulder and squeezed. An almost silent, "Oh, Amy, I'm sorry," escaped his lips.

When Nurse Jane had completed her examination, she nodded to the doctor and left the room. The gray-haired man looked between the two of them and asked, "Things at home going well?"

Amy had the feeling the doctor already knew the answer to that question. Silence reigned as Logan stared at him. The old man shrugged, unperturbed by her brother's reluctance to speak. He picked up the chart at the foot of her bed and glanced through the pages before humphing quietly to himself as if coming to some conclusion.

"Mom and Dad should be back soon; they just stepped out," Logan said, breaking the silence.

Dr. Hauser inclined his head. "That's okay. I can speak to them when they return." He continued his perusal of her chart, glancing sporadically between the two of them.

Logan's placid expression flashed in a mask of devastation. It hurt to see the utter helplessness that shone so clearly in his eyes. Logan had been close to Olivia, too. Growing up, it had been them, the three musketeers—Logan, Amy, and Olivia. Their close relationship had continued as they'd grown, and Amy knew Logan had spoken to Olivia almost as much as he had her. She swallowed hard, deliberately moving her gaze anywhere but at her brother. It met Dr Hauser's. Another pang of remorse pressed her chest as his kind expression dissolved into one of compassion.

"I know a lady, Mildred Miller, who takes in troubled teens at her ranch. I could give her a call," he said.

Logan stiffened. "Thank you, Doctor, but I think we will be all right."

The doctor sighed. "Young man, your sister is a very real danger to herself now. At the ranch, there are people who can help her. She will be safe from harm. I've known Mildred Miller for many years."

Logan shook his head. "I don't think that will be necessary. Amy needs the love and comfort of her family, not a rehab center."

"Why don't we find out what your parents think before any decisions are made? I will recommend to them that your sister go to a rehab center before returning home—for her own safety."

Logan stood in front of the doctor, blocking his movements. Her brother had always been her protector, no matter the circumstance. Had he come home because of her? Or had he heard about Dad?

Dr. Hauser placidly laid his hand on Logan's shoulder and gave it a light squeeze. "Son, I am no threat to you or yours. My main concern is your sister's health and well-being, and these people could help her."

She pulled her covers closer, folding her body into itself, the covers making a cocoon. Her blood pounded through her veins, a headache forming at her temples.

"Why would you want to help my sister? You don't even know us."

The doctor's lips turned up into a smile. "When I was a young man lost to myself, a kind, old man took me in and set me straight. He taught me how to hope and dream. The day I graduated from medical school, I promised myself that I would do the same when someone who needed it crossed my path."

Amy glanced at Logan, who looked back at her, wearing an expression that said, *Is this man crazy?* Amy was sure she wore the same one.

"I'll give you two a bit of time for discussion. I will be back in this ward later today, and you can give me an answer then. Please think carefully."

"Sorry, Doc, but this place your friend has—what's it called?"

"Heavenly Haven." He smiled again, checked something on the chart, and slid it back into the folder at the base of Amy's bed. "It's a horse ranch."

A gentle knock sounded on the door; and a small, brown-haired lady stuck her head in. "Ah, Dr. Hauser, so wonderful to see you."

"Ashley, what a lovely surprise. Who are you here to see today?"

Ashley checked the clipboard in her hands. "I'm looking for Amy Carter."

"Then you're in the right place. If you'll excuse me . . ." Dr. Hauser stood to the side, allowing Ashley into the room, and then he left. Ashley closed the door quietly after he departed and then turned to face Amy and Logan.

"Hi, my name is Ashley Sawyer. I'm from Social Services. I assume you are Amy?"

Amy nodded and said, "This is my brother, Logan."

Ashley was younger than Amy would have expected. Where was the flat hair, haggard face, and bags under her eyes? The air of resignation that followed her like a cloud? Well, that was what all the others had looked like. Ashley was fresh-faced, pretty, and smiled like a lamp was lit up inside her. Maybe she hadn't been in the job long enough to attain those characteristics, based on her obvious youth.

Ashley glanced at Logan and then at Amy. Her eyes went from Amy's messy hair to the white-bandaged arms laying in her lap. Logan reached over and linked their fingers, seeking and giving reassurance.

Ashley confided, "Dr. Hauser would save every kid who walked into this hospital if he could. He's a good man."

"Do you know a place called Heavenly Haven?" Logan asked.

Ashley nodded. "Told you to go there, did he?" She glanced over at Amy.

Amy squeezed Logan's fingers again. "Yeah, he did," she said.

"I would recommend you listen to him. Heavenly Haven is a wonderful place for kids just like you. Logan, could I speak to you outside? Your parents are already waiting. We'll let your sister rest."

Logan nodded. "I'll be right back," he told Amy before following Ashley into the hallway.

Amy closed her eyes and allowed herself to feel the mind-shattering anxiety that was starting to flow through her body. Shivers raced up her spine and shook the bed below her as she tried to suppress the leftover adrenaline. Sleep wanted her, and she felt herself fading into it again. She had to stay awake until Logan was able to tell her what was going on, but she was so tired of it all.

She pressed her eyelids shut and allowed sleep to take her.

CHAPTER FOUR

B rad tipped the small glass of bright green liquid into his mouth, smiling as the alcohol burned its way down his throat. He picked up the half-full tall boy beside him and washed the drink down with a deep swallow of beer. *How many was that?*

He shook his head. It didn't matter; he'd stopped counting around the time the waitress with the low-cut, black tank top had walked past his table for the sixth time. Lucky Harry's didn't care too much about what your driver's license said—only how much money you had, and money was something Brad Thorn had in spades.

He sluggishly lifted his hand to the blonde waitress again, swirling it in the air to signal for another round. The boys from the football team had left a few hours ago, but their company had done little to settle the swirling in his gut. He lifted the beer to his lips again and emptied the contents just as the waitress sidled up to his table.

"Another round?" she asked, pointing to the small, empty glass.

"Yes, please," he slurred, laying another twenty on the table and sliding it over to her waiting hand.

The waitress tested the money, lifting it to the light. Satisfied that it was legitimate, she slipped the note into her waist pack before crossing to the bar. Moments later, she returned, with another small glass of the same green liquid and a brown bottle.

"Max says this is your last round for tonight. He's cutting you off."

Brad acknowledged her words with a quick tip of his head. He lifted the glass to his lips and threw back the liquid, chasing it down with a deep swallow from the brown bottle. That was fine. He was done, anyway. In three long swallows, the brown bottle was empty, too.

Slightly unsteady on his feet, he wandered from the interior of the bar to the dark night outside. The evening had grown quiet; the only sounds to be heard were the owls, the lonely sound of a single car starting, and the bark of a dog in one of the apartment buildings nearby. The evening rush hour was long past, and the road was all but deserted. If he had thought of it, he would have called for a ride, but that would mean waiting, and he was impatient to get home now that the sickness in his stomach lay relaxed in the depths of his alcohol-filled body.

The lights at the front of his dark blue truck flashed to life with a quick press of his fingers. The interior lights blinked just as brightly. He opened the driver's side door and slid inside, his tall body settling into the plush, black, leather interior. The guys always said how lucky he was to have such a great ride, but to him it was just another status statement, courtesy of his father.

The doors closed with a bang, and he pressed the start button, bringing the strong V6 engine to life. For such a powerful car, it was surprisingly quiet, and it drove like a dream—it was so responsive that he hardly had to pay attention to the steering. Ignorant of everything around him, Brad pulled out of the parking space and turned onto Bethel Boulevard, en route to his house.

Lucky Harry's was on the seedier side of Bethel and was therefore a distance from his Clear Spring neighborhood. He preferred it that way. The bar was out of the way enough that no one who knew his father saw him; he wouldn't have to worry about getting into trouble with the law types that seemed to hang on his father's every word. If he wasn't careful, it wouldn't be long until Brad found himself barred from leaving the house—and, possibly, facing armed surveillance.

He hated that his father was so well-known in Bethel, hated the way people looked at him. Their eyes were either disapproving, as if he could in no way measure up to the greatness of his father, or filled with expectation, as if they expected him to do just that. It was exhausting.

When the news of Candice had hit . . . Brad shook his head. He didn't want to think of Candice, didn't want to think of the thick wall of disapproval his father had erected upon the news of her pregnancy. His father had gone deadly silent, his lips pressed into a hard line, white around the edges. And then the lecture had come.

Brad sighed and rubbed his hand over his tired eyes in an effort to keep his wits about him as he drove. The streetlights burning in the evening sky were blurs of streaking lights. The storefronts, now closed for the night, were a smear of luminescent colors, assaulting his eyes.

The traffic light suddenly flickered from green to yellow to red, seemingly quicker than he could keep up with. Brad slammed his foot down on the brake pedal, only to meet the gas instead. Gripping the wheel tightly in his hand, he belatedly tried to bring the truck under control, noticing a dark, hulking mass heading toward him. There was a sharp shriek of metal as the black SUV smashed into his passenger door, pushing him into an oncoming car.

Brad jerked the wheel, trying to correct his trajectory, but it was too late. The large, round oak tree that towered at the intersection in the center of town stood sentinel in his path, showing no mercy to the vehicle heading for it. *Bang.* Glass, plastic, leaves, and branches pummeled his truck like flying debris in the middle of a hurricane as it stopped. The air bag exploded from the steering wheel, knocking him into the black.

What felt like hours later, he came out of his stupor. His head throbbed, and his body ached. There was a high-pitched beeping ringing above his head. He reached up to hit the snooze button of his alarm; but pain stabbed his ribs, and he groaned loudly.

"Oh, you're awake." His father didn't sound all that pleased at the prospect. Blinking, Brad opened his eyes and looked around. His father stood above him, his face creased in disapproval and anger. He opened his mouth but quickly shut it, smoothing out his features and stepping back as a doctor entered the room. Brad snorted. Even that hurt. His father wouldn't be caught dead being so uncontrolled in front of anyone.

"Ah, it's good to see you awake, young man. Brad, is it?" The old doctor had a grandfatherly kind of expression on his face, his eyes filled with such intense kindness and concern that it made Brad's chest hurt.

"Y-yeah, guilty as charged." Brad winced as he took another deep breath.

"You have a few bruises on your ribs from your impact with the tree," the doctor said. "Fortunately, you have good, strong, healthy bones, so there were no breaks, aside from the one on your nose from the airbag. You are a very lucky young man, Brad, to walk away from an accident like that. It could have been fatal."

No doubt, his dad would have rejoiced. Brad glanced at his father to see his reaction to the doctor's news, but his expression remained unmoved. *Figures.*

"When can I get out of here?" he asked, pressing his hand to his side as he tried to sit up.

The doctor stepped forward and adjusted the bed, pressing a pillow behind Brad's back before once again stepping over to his father. "Mr. Thorn."

"Please, call me Adrian."

"Can I speak to you for a moment outside? The nurse will come in to check Brad's vitals while we talk."

With a warning glance over his shoulder, Brad's father followed the old doctor from the room. Brad watched them, noticing what looked like two uniformed officers waiting outside his room. What were they doing here? A tall, pretty nurse with a killer figure entered the room. She gave him an impersonal smile and started checking the machines hooked up to his body. In a few moments, she was done. She wrote something on his file, filled the glass beside his bed with ice chips from a nearby jug, and placed it near his head, resetting the machine beside him.

"Thank you," he offered.

The nurse didn't acknowledge his words. She straightened the blanket over his body, careful not to touch the thick bandages wrapped around his middle, and then exited the room as silently as she had come.

Brad closed his eyes as he waited for his father to re-enter the room. He would probably have plenty to say when there were no witnesses around—and none of it would be good. Brad winced as a cut he hadn't felt earlier pulled at his lips. He was in for it—and this time, he doubted he could talk his way out of it.

CHAPTER FIVE

"Thin is not up for discussion, Brad. It's Heavenly Haven or juvie," his father growled in a low voice.

Brad nodded sullenly and leaned back into the seat of the car with more force than was necessary. His body ached from his brush with death two nights ago, when he and his truck had become uncomfortably well-acquainted with the town square's prized oak tree. He hadn't felt his injuries, drunk as he was. He did now, though.

He clenched his hands into fists, grimacing as the cracked skin between his knuckles stretched and pain shot through the bruises around his body. His face ached, even though the swelling was going down. The doctor said he was lucky to be alive; Brad didn't think so, though.

Working his jaw to avoid another argument with his dad, he closed his eyes and breathed in and out evenly. Heavenly Haven. Who named a juvie center anything close to heavenly? The way his dad described the place, he figured he was in for weeks of hard labor. How was he going to do hard labor when his body ached every time he moved?

"You're lucky I managed to convince George not to press charges after you banged his car up like that. What were you thinking? Wasn't it enough that your license was suspended a week ago?"

George Bainbridge was the mayor of Bethel—and very good friends with Brad's father. He was the only reason Brad was on his way to Heavenly Haven and not the nearest jail.

Brad winced. Two nights ago, he *had*, technically, been driving without a license, after nearly running a walker off the road the week before. And that, added to the DUI—driving under the influence—he couldn't escape juvie. Maybe it would have been better to be locked up; at least then, he wouldn't have to put up with his perfect father.

"Brad, are you listening to me?"

"Yes, sir," he said quietly, waiting for his father to wind down or just leave him alone, but it wasn't to be.

"This is the last time. I can cover up your reckless stunts for only so long." Brad's father owned most of Main Street. That and his generosity to just about any program in the town had earned him the mayor's notice. His father didn't do it for the community, of course—no, it was for the recognition. So, it could be said that Adrian Thorn was a good, upstanding citizen—or, at least, he appeared to be. If only they knew.

Brad chewed on his bottom lip, his thoughts wandering to his mother. He missed her. He wished she was here; maybe she would know what to do—how he could rid himself of the agony ripping his heart and the guilt eating a hole in his gut. But she was gone, taken by cancer when Brad was just a freshman. He swallowed hard. Even after four years, grief lay like a rock on his heart. It was probably better that she couldn't see what a mess he'd made of things.

"I expect you to pull yourself together and behave like a responsible adult when I come to collect you." Brad's father eventually wound down. Brad was a master at paying attention without ever hearing anything. It was an art he'd learned on his visits to his dad's clients and friends: pretending to be the dutiful, perfect son, when most of the time he was dying to go and hide in a place where there were no expectations on him to smile, be gracious, and pretend his mother didn't exist.

The luxurious, black Mercedes pulled to a stop, and his father frowned at the plumes of dust encircling the car. Adrian hated a dirty car.

"Here we are now, Brad . . . "

Brad already knew the lines that would come next. "Yes, I know; I will behave myself, stay away from everyone, and not shame the Thorn name," he said and flung the passenger door open. He grabbed his duffel bag from the backseat and threw himself from the car, not stopping to hear his father's quiet words as the door closed behind him. It might have been *goodbye*—or *good riddance*, for all Brad knew. It didn't matter.

Brad drew a deep breath and stared at the large, brown building before him. What a dump. At this rate, he'd be bedding down with ticks and fleas for the weeks to come. Abruptly, the car revved and slowly withdrew down the long, dusty driveway and back onto the freeway. He almost turned, raced after it, and begged to be taken along—but to where? Jail? The overnight stay after the oak tree was enough to dissuade him that he didn't want to sit in a jail cell for who knew how long. But then, maybe there was the chance of community service?

By the time he'd thought of it, Adrian and the black Mercedes were long gone. Wide expanses of nothing surrounded him, the heat so dense it soaked through his light coat. Did these people even have flushable toilets?

"How can I help you, young man?" A man about as tall as himself approached Brad. He looked like a textbook cowboy—a dark brown Stetson rested above dark, penetrating eyes, a red-checkered shirt covering a wide set of shoulders and jeans. Brad was assuming that's what they were—the pants were so mud-splattered, it was difficult to tell what color they were.

The man was surrounded by a wave of dust. Brad grimaced as the fine, brown powder covered his shoes. He pulled himself up to his full height in an effort to show the man that he was unintimidated by him.

"Brad Thorn. I'm here to serve my time—or something like that."

The man grinned. "Name's Griffin Matthews. I work here at Heavenly Haven."

"Hi." Whatever. Griffin seemed to find something Brad had done amusing because the grin turned into a wide smile. "Why don't I show you your bunk, and we can get started."

"Started? On what?"

"Your sentence, of course," the man said, with a mocking chuckle.

Brad nodded, suppressing his annoyance at this John Wayne wannabe. Carefully side-stepping the mounds of mud, cow refuse, and gravel, he followed the man, grimacing. His shoes would be ruined.

Griffin let out a chuckle and muttered something involving "decent shoes" and "city boy," loud enough for Brad to hear. Heat built under his collar. It wasn't like it was his choice to be in this twice-forsaken place. Wet sand splashed on his legs as they walked, turning the hem of his chinos into a brown, grimy mess. Ugh. What next?

A loud whinny sounded nearby, and Brad glanced to his left. Racing toward them was a rider on a huge chestnut beast, its hoofs digging into the wet earth. A loud whistle pierced the stillness.

The horse reared, slowing before coming to a complete stop—and making the previously stagnant, muddy liquid splash onto Brad's beige-colored chinos and button-up shirt.

"What in the . . . " His hands curled into hard fists, his jaw rigid.

One side look at Brad's expression, Griffin released a loud bark of laughter. "Don't worry; it'll wash."

Brad threw Griffin a sour expression as he lifted a moldy leaf from his shoulder. Griffin unsuccessfully stifled another laugh.

"Come on—let's get you cleaned up and settled in," Griffin said.

He rubbed the horse's large head, speaking quietly to the rider. Brad waited impatiently, ready to change his clothes. When the discussion went on longer than he had anticipated, Brad decided he'd had enough. He guessed he would have to find out where he was staying by himself. He turned, lifting his duffel to his shoulder and shuffling his wet shoes across the uneven ground.

"Brad! It's this way." Griffin laughed again. Brad, feeling murderous, turned and walked in the direction Griffin gestured.

Griffin cuffed his shoulder as he neared and turned him in the direction of a much smaller version of the farmhouse he'd seen earlier. The house looked nice, like a cottage from a fairy tale. It reminded him of his mother. Longing panged in his chest.

"You'll be bunking with me and one of the other guys, but Walter is with his family in Idaho this week, so it looks like it's just you and me for now." Griffin pushed open both the screen and the wooden door behind it, gesturing for Brad to go ahead of him into the dark interior.

Brad blinked as his eyes adjusted to the inside of the cottage. It was surprisingly more spacious than it looked from the outside, and he could see that three rooms branched off from the main living room.

"That's Walter's; that's mine; and that one is your room." Griffin pointed at each door in turn before taking a seat on one of the well-worn couches in the living room. He gestured for Brad to do the same.

Working to mask his shock at the shabbiness of the furniture, Brad carefully lowered himself into a mahogany rocking chair. The chair looked so old and well-used that he was almost afraid it would crack and splinter into a thousand pieces under his weight. It didn't; the chair held firm. It wasn't that the room was dirty. Brad was sure even his housekeeper Mrs. McCleary would be pleased with the cleanliness of it. But it was as if the furniture came from an age long before the man in front of him was born.

Griffin's amusement shone on his face as he looked at Brad. Leaning back into his seat, he rested his ankle on his other knee and settled his hands behind his head. "So, why are you here, Brad?"

"What?" Brad said. "You mean, you don't already know?"

Griffin shrugged and shook his head.

Brad stared at him, aghast. What kind of rehab center was this? "Isn't it your job to know?"

Again, Griffin raised his shoulders and dropped them again. "Things work a little differently at Heavenly Haven than at a traditional healing center. I was informed of your arrival and the reason you were sent here. That's it. Do you want to tell me the rest?" There was a challenge in Griffin's words, but Brad wasn't biting. He dropped his gaze to his hands.

"No," he said quietly.

"All right, then. The sun isn't going to stay up forever, and the chores still need to be done." Griffin pushed to his feet. "Put your stuff away and get cleaned up; I'll wait for you outside to show you to the barn."

"And if I don't?" he challenged.

Leaning against the frame of the door Griffin pegged him with a hard stare. "Brad, this isn't a vacation home; this isn't a place where you can choose or choose not to do something. Every choice you make will have a consequence. How uncomfortable that consequence is is up to you." Griffin's meaning was clear. If Brad chose it, his stay at Heavenly Haven would be anything but pleasant.

He nodded and lifted his duffel to his shoulder. He crossed the carpeted floor to his room, dumped his bag on the neatly made bed, and sank onto its edge. Releasing a deep breath, he looked around the room. *Home, sweet home,* Brad thought sarcastically to himself.

CHAPTER SIX

"Amy, are you ready?" her mother asked, parking the car. Her hands rested on the steering wheel, and she stared out the windshield, waiting for a response.

Amy scanned the open spaces around her. So, this was Heavenly Haven, the place Dr. Hauser had convinced her parents and Logan to send her for the next month. Amy sighed and released her seatbelt, wincing at the tightness of the skin at her wrist. The bandages still clung to her like a second skin, each movement reminding her of the damaged skin below and the neat row of stitches which held it together.

She shrugged. "I guess."

"Honey, we don't need to do this. I'm sure I could convince Dr. Hauser that we could help you at home." Her mother's smile was brave, although there was a hint of panic to it. Dark rings hung below her tired eyes. She'd aged a lifetime in the past five days—Logan, too. It was better that Amy leave and give her mother a break from her problems. It had taken a momentous amount of lying and assurances from Amy to convince Logan to return to school, but in the end, reason had won him over. However, she hadn't seen her father since returning home, and he hadn't said goodbye.

She gently shoved the car door open and climbed out, closing it behind her. Pulling herself up tall, she looked over the roof of the blue sedan at the wide, empty land of the ranch, inhaling the strange mixtures of scents: grass, water, mud, and animals. A farmhouse was to the left of her. It was two stories tall and made of brown timber, with an equally brown wraparound porch. Tall, rectangular windows took up most of the face of the house, broken only by a beautiful, carved wooden door.

On the porch, there were two rocking chairs and three wrought-iron chairs with colorful cushions. She turned around. A large, red barn came into view, and beside it, a white-fenced paddock. The smell of animals grew stronger: horses. And . . . a musty smell made her wrinkle her nose. Dung.

Two beautiful chestnut horses trotted around the paddock, neighing softly to some men nearby. Beyond the paddock was a vegetable garden sprouting with life. Dull white and transparent plastic encased the greenhouses beside it. She closed her eyes, inhaling the tranquility around her, and enjoyed the feeling of the sun on her skin. This place wasn't all bad, but it would take some getting used to.

"Amy?" her mother said from beside her. "This place is breathtaking." There was no mistaking her awe. "I wonder if they have a place for adults here." She sighed softly. "Let's go find out where you need to go." A sign that read *Reception* pointed to the farmhouse.

Amy opened the back passenger door and slung her duffel over her shoulder, anxiety spinning like a top inside her stomach. "Okay, just getting my bag."

Just then, the farmhouse door swung open with a loud clatter, followed by the slight bang of wood as a tall, gray-haired woman dressed in light green capri pants and a bright yellow t-shirt bounced down the stairs. She was plump like a grandma. Soft creases surrounded her twinkling blue eyes, and a wide smile covered her generous mouth.

"Amy Carter, is that you?" she asked, walking up to Amy and pulling her into a tight hug. She repeated the action with Amy's mother.

"I'm Mildred. Welcome to Heavenly Haven."

"I'm Fay Carter, and I guess you already know of my daughter, Amy." Amy's mother gave Mildred a shaky smile, stepped away, and quickly wiped at her cheeks. Amy wrapped her arm around her mother's shoulders and hugged her tightly to her side. This was what she worried about—without her or Logan, who would look after her mother?

"Nice to meet you, Mrs. Carter," Mildred said.

"Please, call me Fay," Amy's mother said.

"Well, honey, you can call me Mildred. Come on, let's go inside. I have some freshly made lemonade and brownies for your arrival."

Amy glanced one more time at her surroundings, not wanting to lose the peace they offered so quickly. Duffel in hand, she followed Mildred and her mother into the coolness of the farmhouse.

"What is it you do at Heavenly Haven?" her mother asked as they entered the quiet reception area. There was no one at the desk, although Amy guessed that was probably where Mildred had just been. Off to the right side was a sitting room. Three brown, leather Chesterfields made a cozy half circle around a round, black coffee table.

On the one wall was an empty stone fireplace. The season for fires was most likely at an end, but Amy imagined what it would be like to sit in front of it during the cold months of the year with a cup of hot chocolate, watching snow trickle down from the sky.

Sadness welled in her chest. She pushed the image away; it reminded her of better times between her mom and dad—like when she was twelve and her family took a skiing trip to Colorado. Her parents had appeared so in love.

There's no such thing, Amy, she thought. Her grip on the handles of her duffel became more and more uncomfortable, until the muscles begged for release.

"Well, Heavenly Haven is more like a working holiday than a therapy center. We have between only two to five young people at a time. We made an exception for Amy because Dr. Hauser is such a wonderful friend of mine and insisted it was what she needed. As it worked out, we have only five young people at the moment, as one decided to depart yesterday against our recommendation."

Her smile dimmed as she turned to Amy. "The next month will be like a break from your normal. Sometimes, a complete removal from a situation can help to renew your mind and spirit." Mildred bustled around the room, placing magazines and books onto nearby shelves as she spoke. "We go to a nearby church on Sundays; and each day, ranch assistants will be tasked with helping around the ranch, caring for the animals, working in the hot houses, and doing whichever other chores they're allocated to."

Ranch work? Really? Amy glanced at her mother, but the expression of relief on her mother's face stopped her from voicing her opinions. Maybe it would be just what they both needed.

Turning her back to the sitting room, Mildred steered them into a room so light, it seemed to be entirely made up of windows. Amy gasped. Sunlight streamed in, flowing onto a multitude of seats spread out across the large, rectangular room. Some chairs were huddled in twos and threes, and others were singular and lonely.

In one corner of the room, there was a large bookshelf packed with books. Amy felt a thrill of excitement. She used to love reading, before there were so many other, better ways to spend her time.

Seeing the names of some of her old favorites instantly made this room the one she liked best.

Beside the first bookshelf, there was another shorter bookshelf lined with black books, their spines all reading *The Holy Bible*. Bible study was a required subject at Bethel Private School, although Amy always did her best to avoid it. Somehow, the words that her teacher Mrs. Vaughn spoke with such passion never moved Amy's heart the way they seemed to move her teacher's. She'd often wondered if there was something in Mrs. Vaughn's tea that made her deliriously happy because she never seemed to have a bad day. Last year, Amy had heard around school that Mrs. Vaughn had lost her husband to cancer—but aside from a two-week absence, Mrs. Vaughn still smiled with the same light as before. Some mornings, her eyes had held the evidence of tears, but somehow, her joy remained. How was it possible?

Shaking herself from her thoughts, Amy joined Mildred and her mother at a neatly set table. She pulled out one of the wooden seats, which had a red cushion, and sat down, dropping her duffel at her feet.

"Amy, would you like some lemonade?" Mildred asked, lifting a large pitcher and pouring the pale yellow liquid into a glass.

"Yes, thanks."

"Fay?"

"That would be lovely, thank you."

As she took a sip of the tangy juice, her phone buzzed in her pocket. She placed the glass on the table and pulled it out. Mildred glanced at her and then at her mother.

"One thing we do require from everyone is that they leave their cell phones in a basket in the kitchen for the duration of their stay." Mildred held out her hand for Amy's phone.

"Why?" Amy asked, reluctantly handing it over. What would she do without her lifeline for a whole month? Mildred stood, walked out of the room, and reappeared a minute later, without Amy's phone.

"Technology is one proven source of depressive feelings among people today. The constant bombardment of pictures and images isn't healthy. Social media show false images of people's lives. They make young people believe they need to be celebrities and athletes with perfect bodies and all the money that those people have to live perfect lives. We've found that the pressure to measure up has caused more than one young person to question his or her worth."

Mildred lifted the plate of brownies and offered them to Amy's mother and then to Amy. "This exercise helps the young person to see past the falseness of these things and to begin to live his or her best life without distractions and influences."

"But what happens when my stay is over? I can't live without my phone for the rest of my life!"

Mildred gently laid her hand on Amy's. "By the time you leave this place, I assure you, you will feel different. And you will have the tools to fight against those influences."

She highly doubted that. Her phone was her life, her connection to her friends and all she was. The bandages encircling her arms caught her gaze, and she swallowed. Perhaps there was some wisdom in what Mildred said.

She allowed her mind to wander as she sipped her lemonade and nibbled on her brownie. The sweet of the chocolate and sour of the lemon was strange but not unpleasant. The conversation between her mother and Mildred faded into the background as she lost herself in the sight of the low mountain range in the distance that surrounded the ranch. Her gaze dipped lower.

One of the horses raced, its rider holding a straw cowboy hat aloft and crying out, his face lit up with happiness. What was it like to be happy? She'd always thought her life was good. She was in with the popular kids; school was going well; and her parents were still together, unlike many of her classmates. Except for hiding her depression, all was okay.

She took a sip of her lemonade, lost in thought. Her extreme spiral down had begun the day Logan had moved to college to begin his first year. A week later, the accident had happened, and the spiral had spun out of control. She sighed.

"Amy, are you ready to see your room?" Mildred asked, drawing her from her morbid musings.

"Sure." There must've been something of her thoughts in her tone because her mother turned and laid her hand over Amy's.

"Are you okay?" she whispered.

"I'm fine," Amy said, with a smile that didn't seem to fool anyone. The worried expression remained on her mother's face. She guessed, in a way, it would always be there; her mother would always worry. It was comforting and annoying all at once.

She hooked her fingers around the handles of her duffel and lifted it to her shoulder, gesturing for Mildred to lead the way. In her other hand, she held her brownie, taking small bites as they filed out of the room one by one.

CHAPTER SEVEN

"**E**very morning, the cows need to be milked, the eggs collected from the hen house, and the horses' stalls cleaned," Griffin said, a half an hour after Brad emerged from the cottage freshly dressed in his oldest jeans and a varsity sweatshirt Candice had given to him for his birthday. He hadn't slept particularly well. The bed was much smaller than his bed at home.

"Before lunch?" Brad asked, sure he must have heard Griffin wrong.

"Yes, the stalls can maybe go till after, but the cows get moody if they're left too long; and the chickens . . . well, they just get cranky when it gets hot."

"Are you serious?"

Griffin laughed and nodded. "If we don't get an early start on chores, we'll still be busy after sundown; and trust me, trying to cut down trees and clear weeds is a lot more difficult by moonlight."

"It takes that long?"

"Yep, this is a big piece of land. Wait till it's time to fix the fences."

Brad blinked hard. Nausea still swirled in his stomach, and he was sure he would heave on Griffin's boots whatever hadn't found its way out of his body the night before.

"There are chores to do every day on a farm this size. The other permanent hands and I take care of the animals on Sunday. And then, of course, we go to church on Sunday."

This was worse than he'd originally thought. Had his father known this when he'd brought Brad to prison camp? Brad snorted. Of course, he did. Why else would he have agreed to this instead of throwing Brad in juvie for the summer? He'd sent Brad away, like the embarrassment that he was. *Like you did with Candice,* a voice said. *Stop it,* he silently berated himself, steering his thoughts away from her and the endless nagging in his gut.

Griffin watched him, concerned. Whatever emotion had flashed across Brad's face at the thought of Candice, he needed to make sure it didn't happen again. He'd done what he'd done, and there was no way to fix it. Carefully arranging his face to what he hoped was a neutral expression, he stared hard at Griffin until he looked away.

"I'd just started on the stalls when you arrived." Griffin handed Brad a tall pitchfork and a pair of rough, hardy gloves. "Put these on, unless you want to have blisters for the next few weeks."

Brad slipped on the gloves and took the fork from Griffin, wincing at the pain that reverberated through his body from the bruises on his back.

"You okay?" Griffin grabbed another pitchfork and walked deeper into the interior of the barn.

"Fine. Let's get on with it, then," Brad said.

The barn was dank inside. The smell was unpleasant, and his stomach lurched. He wouldn't hurl; it wasn't that bad. He could only acquaint the smell with grass—strong-smelling grass—as well as the musky scent of horses. The cloying smells were washed out by a fresh breeze that blew through the open doors. Several long heads hung eagerly over the tops of their stalls, stomping softly as Griffin spoke to each one.

Brad lifted his hand to a tall, dun-colored horse and scrubbed its velvety nose. It'd been years since he'd been near a horse. Horse riding was one of his mother's favorite sports. Often on weekends, they had gone to the stables and rode. Those were good memories—ones he kept close to his chest. Not that it mattered now.

Griffin swung open the door of an empty stall to explain how the stall was to be cleaned. Brad pretended to listen. This was something he already knew; his mother had taught him. The soft alto of her words and the smell of lavender from a nearby bush was one of his favorite memories of her.

"Brad." Griffin tapped his pitchfork against the side of the stall to draw his attention. "Did you get all that?"

"Sure, no problem." He slipped the rough material of the gloves over his hands and gripped the pitchfork tightly.

"Good. Begin here and then do the other four down this side of the barn. When you're done, come find me at the main farmhouse."

Trying his best to ignore the pain in his heart and body, Brad scooped up the first pile of foul-smelling hay and dumped it into a nearby wheelbarrow. When the wheelbarrow was full, he wheeled it outside and looked for a manure pile. Spotting it a short distance from the barn, he drove the wheelbarrow to it, emptied the hay, and returned to the barn. Each swing of the pitchfork burned his wounds, the pain driving his thoughts to the work he was doing and giving him peace from the things he'd rather not think about.

An hour and four clean stalls later, Brad groaned as he straightened. A dull ache ran from the top of his shoulders to his spine and down to his lower back. The watery muscles in his arms protested at any further movement. Brad grimaced. He knew he was fit. At practice, he could run circles against most guys on the football team. Clearly, his well-trained football muscles were not up to the challenge of farm work.

Finished at last, he emptied the wheelbarrow's contents onto the manure heap, parked it in the barn, hung up the pitchfork, and walked tiredly to the farmhouse. What other tortures would he have to endure today?

"You done?" Griffin asked, rising from a barstool in the kitchen as he entered the farmhouse.

"Yeah," Brad said in a strained voice as he lifted his protesting arm to run his fingers through his dusty hair. He needed a shower. Thank goodness he'd seen one on his way out of the cottage. He couldn't wait to stand under its hot spray.

"Great—then we'll get started on the tree clearing."

Wait. What? "More chores?"

"Well, you didn't come here expecting a vacation, did you?"

He kinda had—but at least it wasn't juvie. "But I'm hungry!" He turned to walk outside again and came to an abrupt halt as his eyes landed on a familiar pair of blue ones.

"Amy, what on earth are you doing here?"

Amy stopped dead in her tracks, her pale cheeks turned a sickly white with shock. She opened her mouth a few times to speak, but no words came out. In that space of time, a myriad of emotions raced across her features; he thought he caught confusion, sadness, defiance, and then shame. At last, an older woman came to her side and whispered something into her ear, and the wild panic in her eyes slowly faded. Soft pink color slowly seeped back into her cheeks.

"H-hi, Brad," she said in a small voice. The older woman gently took her arm and guided Amy from the room. Brad stared after the pair. What was Amy doing at a place like this, and why were there white cuffs around her wrists? Last he'd heard, Amy was at Bethel with . . . he stopped the thought right there. He didn't want to think of Willow. He was still furious with her—and himself—after what they'd done to Candice.

Griffin tapped him on the shoulder, handed him a snack bar and a bottle of water, then pushed him out the door. Brad took off his gloves and slipped them into the back pocket of his jeans. He quickly chewed the snack bar and downed the water, following Griffin into a nearby patch of tangled trees. Bare-handed, he grabbed the nearest branch and began to pull on it, ignoring the way the hard, cracked bark cut into his skin.

As the first puncture happened, he considered dropping the branch and telling Griffin what he could do with his afternoon chores, but as the thought crossed his mind, Griffin looked up from his own branch and raised an eyebrow. His words from the morning echoed through Brad's mind—*choices and consequence.*

A part of him didn't care what Griffin might do to him. Didn't he deserve whatever he got? Brad picked up the next branch—a large, mottled green and brown color—and heaved it onto his shoulder. Pain radiated down his arm. Pain was good. A fitting punishment for his crime. And he deserved it all.

"Do you know how to use one of these?" Griffin handed Brad a short-handled axe. Griffin had been chopping a long tangle of branches into smaller, more manageable pieces of wood to be transported to the wood pile behind the main house.

"Don't know," he said and crossed his arms over his chest staring Griffin in the eye.

Griffin chuckled softly. "Want to give it a try, tough guy?" he mocked, holding the blade of the axe handle pointed in Brad's direction.

Brad shrugged. "Suppose so." He took the axe from Griffin, tension winding the muscles in his stomach.

"Just there"—Griffin pointed to a piece of branch between two smaller limbs—"one clean stroke down." He motioned with his hand in a wide arch.

Brad swung the axe hard. It glanced off the wood, flew backward, and landed with a thud in the soft earth.

Griffin's expression remained blank, and thankfully, he stayed silent. He collected the axe, cleaned the blade, and handed it back to Brad. "Try to swing in a straight arc so that you land solidly on the branch. Oh—and maybe try putting those gloves back on, too."

Brad looked down. His hands were filthy. The skin on his palms was a deep red, some patches grazed open from the repeated contact with the rough tree bark.

"Maybe Mildred should take a look at that," Griffin said.

"I'm fine," he said stubbornly, ramming the gloves on. The open wounds stung as they met the coarse fabric, but Brad paid it no mind. He picked up the axe and resumed hacking at the tangled branches.

The sun was low in the sky by the time Brad and Griffin had a neatly stacked pile of logs for the fire and had arranged kindling beside the farmhouse. He'd all but forgotten about his pain in the rhythm of chopping wood and stacking it. His sweater stuck to his sweat-soaked back, and he lifted it, airing his wet skin. It felt good to work hard, despite the pain that lanced through his body at each movement.

"Mildred is calling us for dinner. I think it's time to go and clean up," Griffin said. Brad lifted the hem of his sweater to wipe the sweat

on his face, dropping the fabric as he noticed Griffin's stare. He knew
what Griffin saw—a blotchy mix of purple and green spread like
paint from his biceps and down his abdomen—a reminder of his
brush with death. Griffin raised an eyebrow and pointedly looked at
Brad, who was reluctant to approach the topic. Brad dropped his gaze
and tried to shut down any curiosity Griffin might have.

"It's nothing."

"Really? It sure looks like something," Griffin said.

"What time did you say dinner was?"

Griffin allowed him to change the subject with a small sigh.
"Seven," he said, checking his watch. "Which is about thirty minutes."

"All the time I need," Brad responded with a cocky smile. He put on
the familiar mask of arrogance he wore at school, at football, and any
other time he needed to look surer than he actually felt. It was like he was
another person with another life—one that was perfect, one that had no
dead mother or oblivious father—the life of a person without problems.

With a swagger in his step, he took the gloves off—suppressing
his wince with a smile—and shoved them in his back pocket. When
Griffin didn't try to stop him, he strolled to the cottage and threw
open the door to the room he'd claimed as his own. Only when he'd
closed the door behind him did he let the mask fade.

Brad dropped to the edge of the bed, groaning loudly as his body
settled onto the mattress. Man, it hurt to breathe. He held his hands
closer to his face. Blood and torn skin littered his hands, making
them look like he'd gone three rounds with Mike Tyson rather than
removed a bunch of tree branches.

He clenched his jaw, determined not to be a wimp, as he stood
in search of the shower. There was only one bathroom in the cottage

to be shared by all its inhabitants. The light flickered on with a dull glow as he flipped the switch. Oh, well—old house, he supposed. The tap turned with a squeak, and a powerful gush of water spurted out from the shower head. At least there was one thing in this place that he could look forward to.

Hot water burned his skin as he washed away the muck and blood on his hands. Small peels of skin lifted, and he pulled them off, wincing against the sensations. It hurt more to wash; the soap in the shower hurt almost as badly as the water did. The cuts and open blisters in his palms made it almost impossible to clean himself properly without pain. He pushed on, cursing his own stupidity.

It was a long while later when he finally left the cottage and walked gingerly to the main farmhouse. A happy light shone in the windows. As he got closer, the merriment of voices could be heard from behind the front door. He stood there a while, bracing himself. Who was in there?

Before he could knock, the door swung open; and without a single mocking word, Griffin handed him a tube of ointment, along with a few strips of thick, white bandages. "Rub this liberally on those hands and cover 'em with the bandages. It'll take a few days, but you'll be fixed up soon enough."

Kindness was not an emotion Brad had known often in his world. His chest squeezed at Griffin's gesture. "Thanks."

Griffin grinned and stepped aside, allowing Brad entry to the house. "Come on in."

The sound of laughter greeted their entrance. Brad stalled at the doorway of the wide kitchen, unsure whether he wanted to join the raucous choir of voices. At the center of the large space, a group of teenagers gathered. The preparations for supper were in full swing.

"Come in, Brad. Let me introduce you. I'm Mildred, the owner of the ranch," an older woman said as she rose from her chair. She pointed to a small, red-haired girl with a high ponytail and thick, bottle-rimmed glasses. "That's Bethany." The girl nodded shyly. Next to Bethany was a tall, broad-shouldered boy with brown hair so short he could hardly see the color. "And Alex," Mildred said.

The boy glared at Brad, thick arms crossed over his chest. "Hi," he said.

Brad nodded his greeting.

"Beside Alex is Nathaniel." Only when Mildred mentioned the other boy did Brad see him; it was like the boy was deliberately trying to become one with the faint shadows in the adjoining scullery of the kitchen. Nathaniel didn't say a word—he barely glanced at Brad before hurrying from the room. Everyone stared after him in silence before Mildred heaved a deep sigh. "Griffin, would you . . . " she began.

Griffin nodded and excused himself.

Mildred's gaze lingered on the empty doorway before returning to the last person in the kitchen. "And I believe you know Amy."

"Yes," Brad said, suddenly finding the ability to move. Amy smiled self-consciously in greeting, and he smiled back, walking slowly over to her.

"Hi," he said, sliding his hands into his pockets before remembering what a really bad idea that was. He dropped them to his sides. Amy's gaze shifted to the floor, and an awkward silence descended between them. He wanted to ask what she was doing at Heavenly Haven; but that would beg for his own reason, and he wasn't sure he wanted to talk about that.

Before he could come up with something to say, Mildred clapped her hands loudly. "Grab a seat. It's time to eat."

CHAPTER EIGHT

The tingles started in her hands—just like they always did when the nightmare of those years came alive in her subconscious. Amy's heart rate sped up as her mind fought its way through the smells and sounds. What if someone found out about what he'd done to her? Or how young she'd been when she'd trusted that his words were friendly and he meant her no harm?

Soon, sweat formed, pebbling on her hot skin. She knew waking was the only end to the torment and laughter inside her head, but the nightmare still held her in its grasp.

He walked closer, his hands settling on her shoulders, his face coming closer.

"No, I don't—" Her words were cut off by the hard pressure of him on her mouth, on her body. "No," she tried again, but to no avail. He had her.

Her eyes sprang open, freezing the nightmare in its tracks. Fear held tightly to her body. It would pass soon; it always did. Inch by inch, she regained movement in her limbs. Relief, pure and painful, drove her from her bed and onto her feet.

Breathe, Amy, breathe.

She sucked in full, deep breaths, trying without success to slow her heart rate to something resembling normal.

Breathe, Amy. Breathe.

The attack slowly retreated, and clarity returned to her. She blinked, tiredly flexing her fingers and toes, forcing the blood to flow unhindered. She ran her hands through her hair and walked unsteadily to where her nightgown hung on the back of a round chair. She threw it over her shoulders and secured the belt to her waist.

The nightmares didn't come often anymore. In fact, Amy wasn't sure it had been a nightmare; it was more like a waking dream, where the panic she often suppressed came to punish her for her foolishness. Maybe it was because the secret had never crossed her lips. She kept it locked inside of her, and there, it had grown into the monster she now feared. And the monster would not be so easily ignored—not by alcohol, emotionless hookups, or even drugs. The monster reigned, despite her efforts to tame it.

Curling her hair behind her ears, Amy walked down the stairs to the kitchen, surprised to see a light burning behind the kitchen's closed door. Who was up at this hour? Hesitating to disturb whoever was there, she started to return to her room, only to turn back again. The quietness of her room held no appeal, and she knew if she lay down, the monster would find her again. Tonight, she had no more strength to fight him.

The door swung wide with a near-silent creak as Amy opened it. The quiet figure of Mildred seated at the wooden table in the dining room startled her. Her hands rested on the tabletop, and beside her sat a cup with steam rising from it. Her head was bowed over a book. Her mouth moved silently in prayer.

As Amy turned to leave, Mildred lifted her head, blinking slowly before turning to face her.

"Couldn't sleep?" Mildred asked. Her expression was open and welcoming. Amy shook her head and slowly closed the distance between them.

"I don't sleep well."

"Would you like some warm milk?" Mildred pointed to her mug, lifting it in Amy's direction.

"No, thanks. I don't really like milk. It hurts my stomach."

"Oh, dear. Are you lactose-intolerant?"

"No, it's only . . . after . . . " Amy sighed. How did she explain the sick feeling in her stomach without telling Mildred everything that had happened to her?

Mildred's gaze traveled her face. No doubt, she noticed Amy's flushed cheeks, the sheen of sweat on her forehead, and the rapid pulse still beating at her neck.

Amy's breath caught in her lungs as Mildred stood and walked over to her. She stared at Amy for a long moment and then hesitantly drew Amy into a hug. She didn't say a word, just held her. It felt good just to be held, like a mother holds a daughter. Her mother hugged her, but there had to be a reason; and sometimes, Amy didn't realize how much she missed that motherly hug until she was hugged again.

She let herself lean into it, and the prick of tears burned her eyes. Soon, rivulets were running down her cheeks. If Mildred felt the wetness against her night gown, she didn't mention it. She just held Amy while she wept.

When Amy had cried herself out, she pulled out of Mildred's arms and wiped her face, reaching for a box of tissues on the kitchen counter. She couldn't lift her eyes to Mildred; surely, the woman would ask a question that Amy refused to answer.

"Better?" Mildred asked, moving back to the table again and picking up her mug. She took a sip and then walked to the kettle and flipped the switch. "How about cocoa?"

What does it matter what I drink? Amy mused. *There will be no more sleeping tonight anyway.* "Thank you," she said, still unable to meet Mildred's inquiring gaze. Should she tell her what happened? Would Mildred believe her? But maybe Mildred would know how to drive the monster away.

The kettle clicked off with a loud smack, startling Amy. Mildred made the cocoa, and then she gestured to the table where her own cup rested. "Come sit."

Unease crawled up her spine. She wasn't ready. She rolled her shoulders, trying to ease the tension from them.

"I think I'll just . . . " Amy lifted her head, and the words froze in her chest at the soft compassion in Mildred's eyes. "Okay," she said, changing her mind. She pulled the chair from under the table and sat to the left of Mildred.

"Amy, I'm not going to ask you any uncomfortable questions. I am more than willing to give you the space you need until you are ready to share your story. Let me say this: a burden shared is a burden halved. I know it sounds like a silly old proverb, but sometimes, when we get the courage to let others know about our troubles, they become easier to bear."

Amy blew her nose and wiped the remaining moisture from her eyes. She clasped her unsteady hands around the warm mug, relishing the warmth soaking into her cold hands.

"Thank you, Mildred. I think I'll just drink my cocoa on the porch and then try again to get some sleep."

Mildred smiled, her expression kind. "Good night, Amy. I hope you get some sleep soon." Mildred sipped at her own mug and returned to her reading.

Amy quietly slipped out into the cool evening, inhaling the comforting smell of grass and horses. It was so quiet that she could hear the shuffle of her feet across the porch planks. She froze. There were another set of footsteps. She was not alone. For a moment, she thought it was Alex. He had taken a liking to her and was persistent, despite her refusal to talk to him. She wasn't here to find a hook-up, but Alex seemed to think otherwise.

To her left, a shape moved on one of the rocking chairs; it was a man, lifting a bottle to his mouth. The chair creaked, and each movement cut into the still night. He was tall, and there was something familiar about the set of his jaw and the shadow of his profile. Did she know this man? Who did he remind her of?

The man lowered the bottle and faced her. His blue eyes were unfocused and confused as they met hers. It was Brad. Their conversation had been stilted and impersonal earlier at dinner, like they weren't sure if they should acknowledge knowing each other.

"Amy." Brad rose unsteadily to his feet. Had he always been this tall? she wondered, looking up at him. She was five feet, three, but in the darkness, he seemed enormous. And yet, despite the darkness and the awkwardness of the situation, it was comforting to see him.

"Brad, what are you doing here?"

"I could ask the same of you." His words were slurred.

"Summer vacation," Amy said, thinking on her feet. "You?"

A smile cracked the side of Brad's mouth. "I was in the neighborhood." There was no way that was possible. Heavenly Haven was a three-hour drive from Bethel. She guessed neither of them felt particularly like sharing.

"What's that?" He moved closer, and the smell of alcohol burned her nose. Was he drunk?

"Cocoa. Want some?"

Brad shook his head. "Nah, I got my own," he said, and lifted his bottle to his mouth. He chuckled and then stumbled, tripping over the potted plant and crashing to his knees. The lights in the main house turned on, one by one.

CHAPTER NINE

A deep baritone pulled Brad to wakefulness. Where was he? And why was there a strange man hovering upside down above him?

"Brad, can you hear me?" Griffin asked as he hooked his hands under Brad's shoulders and hauled him to his feet.

He wobbled unsteadily, coming dangerously close to greeting the ground before Griffin roughly righted his balance.

"Easy does it," Griffin said. His expression was a mixture of compassion and anger.

Brad rubbed his hand down his chest to his belly to calm the wave of sour bile rising up his throat.

"Leave me alone. I can lie here."

Griffin shook his head. "No, you can't. Come on, kid. Let's get you somewhere you can sleep it off."

Well, if Griffin insisted . . . "Okay."

Griffin dragged him back to the cottage, his brawny arm firm around Brad's waist. Once they were inside, he lowered Brad onto the bed.

"Thanks," Brad muttered before his surroundings faded into nothing.

The painful throbbing in his temples woke Brad. He groaned loudly and covered his eyes with his forearm to block out the piercing sunlight. *Where am I?*

He scanned his surroundings, and then he remembered—Heavenly Haven. He was in his room. The door was open, and through it was a clear view of Griffin asleep on the sofa. Why wasn't he in his bed?

He sighed loudly and suppressed a groan as dizziness swirled in his head and light pricked his swollen eyes. Nausea crawled up his chest as he stumbled into the bathroom. He held it off long enough to reach the toilet before losing the contents of his stomach.

"Ah, you're awake," Griffin said, rising from the sofa with a loud yawn and moving to the bathroom doorway. The early morning sun shone in an eerie, colorful silhouette behind his wide shape.

What did Griffin want? Brad grimaced and shut the door in his face. He needed a shower. The water was blessedly hot as it had been the night before. It drove the alcoholic fog from his brain and eased the constant throbbing behind his eyes. When the water began to cool, Brad turned off the tap. Walking from the bathroom to his room, he dressed quickly. He would have to face Griffin sometime.

Griffin waited on the sofa for him. The empty bottle of Jack stood on the small coffee table. Unable to meet Griffin's questioning gaze, Brad turned to the bar fridge, grabbed a bottle of water, and chugged it down. A bottle of Tylenol appeared before his face, and he gratefully took the two proffered to him and slugged them down with another bottle of water.

"Ready to tell me your tale?" Griffin asked. He didn't look angry. Why wasn't he scolding Brad? Or telling him how useless he was—or something? Instead, understanding lingered in Griffin's deep-set eyes.

"It's no big deal. Just a habit."

"It's more than that. You and I both know it."

He watched Brad, as if expecting him to agree. Brad didn't reply; he only stared back. He didn't know Griffin from dirt. Why would he care what Brad had done? How would he know how to deal with the regret that bred like a sickness inside him? And yet, he wanted to trust Griffin and tell him about Candice. But Griffin, like his father, wouldn't understand. So, why bother?

"Aren't you going to throw me out?"

Griffin frowned and nodded slowly. "I could. But the question is, do you want me to?"

It was Heavenly Haven or juvie—wasn't that what his dad had said? Brad thought back to the night he'd spent incarcerated after his license had been suspended. He shuddered. "No."

"Then you have some hard choices to make. I guess I don't need to tell you that if you are caught inebriated on the farm again, you will be sent home."

Brad dropped his gaze to his muddy shoes and nodded. Juvie definitely would be worse than having to drag a few tree branches.

Griffin rose and clapped Brad gently on the shoulder. He disappeared into his room, closing the door behind him. A moment later, he came out and handed Brad a book. It was heavy and had a black cover. "This might help you make the right choice."

Brad took the book from Griffin and snorted. He'd had enough of the Bible to last a lifetime. At school, everything was "the Bible this, Jesus that." What did God know about his regrets and mistakes? Better question—why would He care?

"Thanks, but no thanks," Brad said, handing the Bible back to Griffin.

"Hang onto that. You never know when you might need it."

Fat chance, Brad thought, as he took it with him into his room. He never opened a Bible—unless forced to by a teacher. He glanced at the gold-embossed writing on the cover and tossed the Bible into his duffel. He didn't need some ancient book that was hardly relevant. Maybe Griffin was the one who'd had too much to drink, not him. He left the room without giving the Bible a second thought.

"You ready?" Griffin waited for him at the front door of the cottage, his Stetson on his head and ready to go to work.

Figures. Of course, he wouldn't allow Brad to wallow in his room with his aching head and his guilty conscience. He almost told Griffin to go ahead without him, but he figured Griffin wouldn't let him stay behind.

A short walk later, they entered the farmhouse for breakfast. Voices filtered into the sunlit hallway, and one in particular caught his ear. Amy. A vague memory circled in his mind before disappearing like the early morning mist.

As they entered the dining area, the smell of breakfast filled his nostrils, and his stomach roiled. Still, he approached the buffet, where Amy was reaching for the plate of toast. Mildred had laid out a breakfast fit for a king across a large, wooden table that seemed to take up most of the room. Eggs, bacon, pancakes, apples, strawberries, and bananas were piled high on white plates. Beside those were urns of strong, black coffee and some funny-smelling herbal tea.

"Hi," he said hesitantly.

"Hi. We have to stop meeting like this," she said. Brad turned his gaze to hers, thinking she meant the greeting as a reprimand, but the soft smile lingering at the side of her pink lips took the thought away. She was joking.

"Yeah, I guess." Hungry was something he was not this morning—but the thought of spending the whole day doing hard labor on an empty stomach had him reaching for a few strips of bacon, a large scoop of eggs, and the biggest coffee mug placed beside the urn. When his plate was full, he nodded to Amy and then sought the quiet of the morning. The noise in the house did nothing for the pounding in his temples. He hoped the pills would kick in soon.

Once outside, he chose a black wrought-iron chair beside a stout, glass-topped table and set his plate down. The iron was cold like the morning air and gave off a faint metallic smell. He sat; at least, the bright blue cushions were soft.

The screen door slapped open, and Amy walked out. She smiled shyly and gestured to the chair opposite him.

"Do you mind if I sit?" she asked.

"Sure, help yourself."

They ate in companionable silence until Amy cleared her throat. "So, you're missing out on senior year, too?"

Brad paused his fork half-way to his mouth. He set it down. "Yeah, I couldn't deal with drama anymore," he said, sarcasm dripping from every word. Amy frowned and nodded. When she didn't reply, his curiosity got the better of him. "Why are *you* missing out on our senior year? I thought you'd be neck-deep with Felicia, planning an epic end-of-the-year blowout or something."

"Me, too," she said softly. Her gaze wandered to the white cuffs peeking from underneath her red, long-sleeved t-shirt as if in answer.

He followed her gaze, wondering. Did the bandages have something to do with why she was there? As far as he knew, Amy was doing fine at school. She had a great family, did okay socially. He didn't know her exact grades, but she didn't seem to spend any time in study hall, like he was forced to do. Did he dare ask? Swallowing his bite of food, he took a sip of his coffee. "What are you doing here, Amy?"

"I suppose I could ask you the same question."

Brad nodded. He wasn't any readier to spill his secret than Amy was.

Amy swallowed hard and took a sip of her coffee. "Does your being here have anything to do with why Candice suddenly left school in the middle of the semester?" She studied him expectantly. His food lodged like a giant boulder in his throat.

There weren't many people who knew all the sordid details of what had happened between him and Candice and Willow. It hurt to know that she knew. The mistakes he'd made with Candice had unfolded like a giant pyramid falls—piece by piece. And this particular pyramid had exposed his bleeding heart to everyone. It was gut-wrenching. He was such a fool, thinking only of himself while Candice, who'd loved him and stood by him, carried the weight of their decision and actions alone.

And then there was Willow—she'd played him, told him he'd done the right thing. He shouldn't have listened to her lies. When he'd realized Candice was gone and wasn't coming back, a part of him had broken, and the wound still bled. How would he ever get past the regret of his choices and the shame that he hid from everyone except himself?

He didn't want to answer, but what would it help to lie? "Yeah."

"I'm sorry, Brad," Amy said, glancing up to meet his gaze.

Not half as sorry as he was. Amy sipped her coffee, her gaze never leaving his. Did she understand? Or was that just wishful thinking? Probably the latter.

"What about you? What deep, dark secret brought you here?"

Amy's porcelain complexion paled further, so much so that Brad thought she might keel over at any moment. He looked down at her long sleeves again. As Amy took another bite of her breakfast, her sleeve rode up to expose a long piece of white bandage, which ran from the crease of her wrist and disappeared into her sleeve. A deep red filled Amy's cheeks as her eyes followed his to her arm, and she quickly dropped her knife and fork and pulled the sleeves down around her knuckles.

"Nightmares."

She took her plate and utensils in hand and hurried back into the house, leaving Brad watching her retreating figure.

CHAPTER TEN

Escape was always the best course of action when Amy found herself in an uncomfortable situation. Her heart thrashed like thunder in her chest, spurring her feet faster into the house. Tremors shook her hands so badly that the plate tipped dangerously and almost fell to the floor. She should have expected her conversation with Brad to eventually turn to the reasons she was at the farm. After all, she'd all but asked him to question her.

Taking another deep breath, Amy dumped the rest of her food in the trash and placed her plate into the dishwasher. Her appetite was gone. Her stomach was already filled with rocks. What did Brad think of her being here? What conclusion did he come to when he saw the bandages on her arms? Did he know? She was sure he did. The hint of understanding and compassion she'd seen as she had walked away from him said he'd come to the right conclusion about why she was at Heavenly Haven instead of living out her final year of school in spectacular fashion.

"Amy, are you all right?" Mildred bustled into the kitchen with an energy Amy was coming to recognize as her normal. Mildred was always light on her feet, despite her age and size. She flitted gracefully from one place to the next, her motions reminding Amy of a ballet she had once seen with her mother. Dad and Logan had refused to go, so Amy and her mother got to spend an evening basking in the delight of the arts.

She wondered how her mother was doing with the separation. Had Logan come home after all? And what of her father? Was he sorry yet for what he'd done to their family? Worry beat like a drum in her chest, and she felt the familiar speeding of her blood through her veins, telling her a panic attack was on its way.

"I'm fine," she lied, sidestepping Mildred and making for the door. She saw Brad glance up to watch her as she hurried outside, down the porch steps, and into the open. She trotted over the uneven ground but didn't run. Running would make her determination to flee obvious, and she just wanted to be alone to gather her thoughts.

Clean morning air filled her lungs with hints of straw, dung, and the sweet smell of flowers from the nearby bed as she traversed the uneven ground to the nearest corral. It was early, and most of the horses were still in their stables. A lone horse neighed, shaking its mane and trotting around the corral. It was a beautiful animal and so tall, it loomed over her, its liquid eyes soft. The horse was as black as the night. Small patches of brown and white dotted its majestic body as he stopped his trotting, shaking his great head before walking in long, graceful steps to where she stood.

Amy held out her hand and waited for the horse to come closer. The horse shook his great head again and then moved closer to nuzzle at her palm. The soft velvet of his nose tickled her skin. She trailed her hand from the horse's nose up his face and scratched the fur behind its ears. Slowly, the gallop of her heart calmed, and air expanded in her lungs. It was quiet. The only thing she could hear was the gentle beat of her heart—and the sound of approaching footsteps.

"Did you do that?" Brad asked, pointing to the bandages. "Did you try to kill yourself?"

A cold shiver raced up her spine as she ran her shaky fingers over the spongy surface of the bandage. What could she say? Settling on the truth, she lifted her gaze to his and nodded.

Compassion filled Brad's blue eyes. "Did it hurt?" he asked, coming to a stop beside her. He folded his muscular arms across the top of the corral fence and rested his chin on them.

"I don't remember." Truthfully, the only thing she remembered about that awful night was seeing him outside the bathroom and waking up in the hospital. Dr. Hauser said somewhere in her subconscious, she remembered, but so far, the memory had yet to surface. Maybe the dreams were the memory trying to come out; Dr. Hauser had said that was possible. She ran her hands over the horse's mane again, seeking its rough texture.

"When did it happen?"

Amy's hand clenched involuntarily around the horse's hair. She forced her muscles to relax, and she slid her fingers through the length of the mane, soothing herself. Although her heart did not race with fear anymore, anxiety still shot through her, heating her limbs with tingles of lightning. "A week ago, at Felicia's house."

Brad's lips thinned. "I'm sorry, Amy. I had no idea you felt that way."

"Nobody did." She blew out a heavy breath. "I didn't tell anyone how bad I really felt." She drew a deep breath to clear her thoughts. "Olivia, my cousin, died; Logan left for college; all that stuff happened with Willow and Candice. One thing after the other . . . "

She knew the instant she'd said something wrong because a change came over Brad. He went rigid at her side, heartbreak morphing his feature. *Ah.* He'd told the truth earlier.

Forgetting her own pain and torment, she reached over and laid her hand atop Brad's. "I didn't . . . I'm sorry."

Brad worked his jaw so hard, she thought she might hear his teeth split at any moment. Feeling foolish for offering her support, she tried to withdraw her hand and was surprised when Brad held fast to it.

"You have nothing to be sorry about. I messed up. I just . . . " He swallowed hard. "I wish I could . . . " The sound of oncoming footsteps interrupted whatever he would have said next.

His face blanked into a neutral expression. He dropped her hand as Griffin and Mildred joined them at the corral.

"Do you know how to ride, Amy?" Mildred asked, patting the side of the horse's head.

"No. I always wanted to." The thought scared her to death, but she wouldn't tell Mildred that.

Mildred smiled. "Well, if your work in the stalls today gets done quickly, Griffin would be happy to take you on a few trips around the corral."

Griffin nodded and smiled politely at Amy. When she'd first seen the older man, he'd scared the life out of her. He was huge and wide-chested and had a rough edge. But as the conversation had carried over last night's dinner, he'd been kind to Bethany when she had dropped her drink, gently taking the broken glass from her hand and helping her clean up the grape liquid like there was nothing he would rather be doing. Alex had gotten into a raucous discussion with Brad about football that had almost ended in blows, but Griffin had calmed the two with a firm hand and a patient tone. He was respectful to Mildred and treated each of the teens with equal thoughtfulness and sincerity. Griffin was what her mother referred to as a "good guy," which eased her fears considerably.

"Stalls?"

Mildred smiled. "I see you have a natural affinity with the horses, so you'll work in the stalls today with Griffin and Brad."

Amy swallowed hard. "Mildred, I think . . . " She trailed off, sweeping her hand down her arm to her wrist in explanation. Wouldn't the hard work of cleaning stalls cause her stitches to come undone?

Mildred's expression gentled. "Only do what you feel you can, Amy; but I know you're capable."

Doubtful, but it didn't look like she had a choice. "But maybe put on more suitable clothing first."

Amy glanced down at her beige capri pants, red shirt, and flats. "I think you're right."

"Join Brad and me whenever you're ready," Griffin said, beckoning for Brad to follow him.

Brad glanced back at her, gave her a brave smile, and followed Griffin into the barn.

Amy smiled back. She hoped it was encouraging in some way to Brad. The sadness in his blue depths made her heart bleed in sympathy for him. It must be so hard for him. And what of Candice? Amy could only imagine what she must be going through. Suddenly, her part in Candice's alienation became clear, and her body grew hot, mounting on top of the loathing she already felt for herself.

Brad and Willow hadn't been the only ones to treat Candice like a social pariah when news of her pregnancy broke. Sadly, she had, too. Regret compounded on guilt, compounded on shame. It was too much. Tears filled her eyes, and she swallowed them back, pushing those thoughts to the back of her mind.

"How are you this morning, Amy?" Mildred asked.

Amy bit her lip. "Fine, I guess." Her emotions were too near to the surface for this to be the truth. She hurt for Brad, for Candice, for herself, and for the unfairness of life. Mildred nodded, falling in step with Amy as they made their way back to the farmhouse.

"Tell me about your family, Amy."

"Not much to tell. I have an older brother, Logan. My dad's gone, and my mom—I hope she's okay without me there."

If her blunt words surprised Mildred, the woman didn't show it; nor did her face harden. It remained the same—interested.

"Do you feel responsible for your mom?"

Did she? Maybe not *responsible*, but she wanted to be there for her. She didn't like to see her mother in pain. "No, but I'm sure my being here can't be easy for her. I mean, she just found out my dad cheated on her again; and Logan has school; and my grandparents are so far away. Who's going to be there for her—to help her?"

Mildred stopped Amy with a hand on her arm. "Amy, what about you?"

"What about me?" Didn't Mildred understand? She didn't matter— not when there were others suffering so much more than she was.

Mildred lightly took Amy's hands into hers and turned them palms-up to show the white bandages. The stitches itched, but Amy chose to ignore them; they were still a reminder of what she'd done. Mildred looked into her eyes. "Do you believe that all things in life work out for a reason?"

"I suppose, but what could be the reason for me being here, my family falling apart, my friends . . . " She stopped. She didn't want to think about her friends at the moment. She was a terrible friend.

"It says in Romans 8:28, 'And we know that in all things God works for the good of those who love him, who have been called according to his purpose.'"

"But I don't believe in God—how can any of this be for a purpose?"

Mildred shrugged. "I'm not sure, Amy, but I do believe you *are* here for a reason—and maybe the reason is simply for your mother to see a need for God in her own life. Maybe it's only for you to find God yourself. No matter what it is, there is always a purpose. God doesn't allow us to go through trials for no reason."

Unsure of the truth of Mildred's words, she shrugged, admitting, "I guess."

"Come. Let's see about your clothes; those stalls won't wait forever," Mildred said kindly.

The thought of God knowing her and having a purpose for her life was confusing—and more than a little troubling.

CHAPTER ELEVEN

Up and over, Brad thought, poking hay onto to the pitchfork and then dumping it into the wheelbarrow. The monotonous movement kept Brad's mind off the pain in his tired body. He hadn't slept well, thanks to his alcohol-induced stupor. His head throbbed.

Heat burned his neck as snippets of the past night blew across his memory. The vague recollection of being dragged back to the cabin by Griffin kept his eyes firmly focused on his task as Griffin walked by. When he did find the strength to lift them, Griffin's gaze solemnly met his own. Why wasn't he angry?

Griffin suddenly stopped shoveling hay and straightened with a loud sigh. "How's the head?"

Brad groaned and planted his fork into the nearest pile of hay. "Fine." He swallowed, rubbing the back of his neck and staring at something over Griffin's shoulder as he made the decision to speak. "I, uh . . . want to apologize for last night."

"Are you apologizing because you feel ashamed of your behavior or because you're genuinely sorry and want to change it?"

Why was he apologizing? He always apologized after he'd done something wrong. It had been nailed into him. But there was one thing he would never get the chance to apologize for—and how he wished he could. "A bit of both, I guess," he said.

"Brad . . . " Griffin trailed off. His gaze focused on something behind Brad.

Brad turned around. Amy stood at the entrance of the barn, looking lost. Her blue eyes flickered between him and Griffin before they dropped to her feet.

"Mildred sent me." Amy's dark, shoulder-length hair was held back by a red, paisley bandanna. She was every inch a cowgirl, complete with a well-worn, green-checkered shirt and jeans.

"Hey, nice outfit," he said, forcing a smile.

Amy lifted her gaze to his and wrinkled her nose. "Same to you," she said, gesturing to his dirt-soaked jeans and t-shirt.

He shrugged. These were his clothes, designer labels and all. What would his father think if he could see Brad now? His expensive clothing soiled, he was decked out like a lowly farmhand, instead of the son of one of the most prominent people in the town of Bethel. He snorted. It was probably a good thing that his father wasn't here to see him.

"Do you know how to clean a stall?" Griffin handed Amy a pair of thick gloves and a pitchfork. He gestured to the stalls lining both sides of the barn, where a tapestry of color hung over the stalls.

"No."

"Brad seems to have a handle on it. Why don't you show her how?"

"Sure." He felt the weight of Amy's gaze on him as he moved around the stall, explaining the intricacies of stall-cleaning. He heaved the hay into large piles and loaded the heap into the wheelbarrow. "And finally, you take the wheelbarrow and dump the dirty hay on the pile beside the barn," he finished. He took off his gloves, wiped his sweaty brow with his sleeve, and slid his hands into his back pockets.

"You want to give it a try?" Griffin asked Amy.

"Sure." Gripping the pitchfork firmly between her hands, Amy walked to the next empty stall and opened the gate.

Brad followed. As Amy hesitantly plunged the pitchfork into a dirty heap of hay, Brad began on the pile beside her. "How are you feeling today?" he asked in a low voice.

Amy glanced over her shoulder at Griffin, who was busy in the stall beside them. "Okay—you?" she whispered back.

"Could be better." He shrugged.

They lapsed into silence as they worked, both lost in their own thoughts. In short order, the stall was clean. Amy rested her pitchfork against the stall wall, groaning as she straightened.

"Sore?" Brad asked.

Amy nodded. "I don't know if my mom read the brochure before sending me here. I didn't know torture was part of the picture."

A dry laugh rose from his chest. "I wouldn't go that far." He stretched his arms, wincing as the muscles in his back and arms protested the movement. "I do know that a bit of exercise never hurt anyone."

"Says the guy who can't walk without wincing. What's with that, anyway?"

Brad's smile slipped. He lowered his gaze to the floor before answering, "Just the reminder of one stupid decision after another."

"I know what you mean . . . " Brad lifted his head. Amy's head was bowed, focused on her bandaged wrists. "But it seemed like the only choice at the time, right?"

"Yeah, at the time." That was how it was with both Candice and Willow. His relationships joined the long list of poor decisions he'd made in the years since his mother had left him all alone—since his father had turned into more of machine than a father. He tried to push the heaviness from his throat, but it would not be moved. It sat there like a weight, demanding he take notice of it. Did he deal with it? Would that bring him peace?

"Amy, here you are—I've been looking for you." That neanderthal Alex lumbered into the barn and made a beeline for Amy. "Mildred asked me to come and get you. She needs you in the house." Brad doubted that Alex had even noticed his presence.

"Oh, okay. Thank you, Alex. I will be there in a minute. Brad and I just need to finish the other stall."

Alex glanced around the barn, his eyes widening slightly at the sight of Brad standing less than a foot away from Amy. He glared at him, crossing his arms over his impressive chest and leaning against a closed stall. "I'm sure he can manage by himself. He seems strong enough." He sneered.

Heat flashed through Brad at the obvious challenge. Who was this guy? Feeling the unfamiliar urge to move Amy behind him to protect her, he stepped closer to her side and got to work. This time, the cleaning took far longer, but judging by the intense looks Alex often cast in Amy's direction, the boy had a thing for his friend.

Amy was rigid beside him, her hands shaking slightly as she lifted the pitchfork up and down. Alex made her uncomfortable. As soon as the stall was clean, Brad took the gardening tool from Amy and leaned it against the stall wall, slinging an arm around her shoulder as he guided her from the stall. She stiffened and then relaxed.

"Let us just tell Griffin we're done, and then we'll come over to the farmhouse," he said to Alex, dismissing him.

Alex's face hardened. "She doesn't know where Mildred is, so I was told to bring her."

"Ah. Well, I think I'll walk with you back to the house, Amy. I wanted to get a drink, anyway."

Amy's relief couldn't have been more evident. Brad dropped his arm as they left the shadows of the barn and walked over to where Griffin was mending a fence by the pig pen.

"Griffin, if you don't mind, I'm gonna walk with Amy and . . . " He looked at the gorilla beside Amy. "Alex, was it? And find something to drink. Can I get you anything?"

"Nah, I'm good. Hurry back; the rest of this fence isn't going to mend itself," Griffin said as he waved them off.

"Sure." Moving closer to Amy's side, he walked in step with her and her hovering shadow, only moving from her side when Alex broke off from them and lumbered over to the crop storage barn. John and another of the workers waited for him there.

Once Amy was safely in the kitchen with Mildred, Brad returned to Griffin. He found him beside the chicken coop, inspecting the chicken run for holes.

"All done with the other pen?" he asked, pulling on his gloves and taking a set of needle nose pliers offered by Griffin.

"Not yet. I came to check on this one to see how much more wire I need. It looks like there are a few holes here that will need to be mended to protect the chickens. I need to get back to the workshop to collect more wire."

"Where is it?"

Griffin tipped back his Stetson and rubbed his forehead. "In the barn beside the tack room, you should find a smaller room that will have what we need."

Brad followed Griffin back into the dim interior of the building and into a small office-like space at the back. The walls were lined with tools, which hung between well-placed nails and wooden shelves rising up from the floor to the height of his waist. Every tool known to man was on display.

From the corner of one of the shelves, Griffin pulled a large box filled with various-sized wire rolls. He lifted two and showed them to Brad. "This one is for the pig pen," he said of the ball on the right, "and this thinner, more versatile wire is for the chicken coop." He handed both balls to Brad and returned the box.

"Can I ask you something?" Brad asked as they walked back to the pig pen.

"Sure."

"What you asked earlier—about drinking? It sounded like you spoke from experience or something." They continued from the barn, walking along the path back the way they'd come.

Griffin paused and rubbed the back of his neck. He settled on his haunches beside the pig pen and gestured for Brad to do the same.

"That's because I got drunk pretty often once, too."

Brad glanced up in surprise. "You did?"

"It was a long time ago. I was much younger and angrier."

"At what?"

"Anything and everything. I was angry at life, and I decided would take it out on anything and anyone who gave me trouble." Griffin's face relaxed, lost in a faraway memory. "When I was a college freshman, my buddy, Mac, and I were in a terrible car wreck. Mac was killed. I was lucky and ended up in hospital under Dr. Hauser's care." His voice dropped to a low whisper. "I will forever be grateful for that day because without it, I would have walked my last steps on this earth long ago."

"What happened?" Brad asked, taking the proffered string of wire from Griffin's hand. He watched as Griffin twined the wire between the two prongs of the pliers and then wound it between the gap in the pig pen's fence.

"That, I think, is a discussion for another time."

"Why?"

Griffin sighed. "Because, Brad, sometimes it takes a dramatic event to get our attention. In your case, the event has already happened. Maybe, for you, it will take a more subtle approach for God to reach you."

"Or maybe God thinks I'm not worth saving."

Another sigh escaped Griffin. He took off his gloves and rested one hand on Brad's shoulder. "That is where you are wrong."

Griffin returned his gloves to his hands and busied himself with fixing a large tear in the pig pen's fence.

A verse he'd heard once in Bible class slipped into Brad's mind. *"For this is what the Sovereign Lord says: I myself will search for my sheep and look after them"* (Ezek. 34:11).

Was God looking for him? Was He trying to get his attention? Did He really care what was happening in Brad's life? How could He? Questions circled his mind for the remainder of the morning as he and Griffin moved from the pig pen back to the chicken coop and then onto a small section of fence surrounding the vegetable gardens. The sun was hot, the heat burning the tender skin along his collar and the tips of his ears.

When lunchtime came, the sun was high in the sky. Brad took a deep swallow from his water bottle, washing the dust from his mouth and then emptying the remainder of the bottle over his head. The cool water felt like heaven as it dribbled from his head to his shoulders and soaked his shirt. He was tired and filthy, although that didn't subdue the feeling of accomplishment bursting in him after the day's work.

Smiling, he wondered if Amy was still in the farmhouse and if he could sit with her for lunch.

CHAPTER TWELVE

Amy rolled her stiff shoulders, pulling in a few breaths. The coolness of the farmhouse blew out at her as she opened the front door and walked inside. She stopped herself from glancing over her shoulder at Brad. It was nice of him to walk with her. She didn't know why she felt so uneasy with Alex. There was something about the way he held himself that reminded her of someone she'd rather forget. Shaking out her sore hands, she crossed the room to the kitchen.

"Amy, dear, are you all right? You're as pale as sheep's wool." Mildred hurried around the counter and wiped her hands on a dishtowel before thrusting it back into the pocket of her apron. Her arms wrapped around Amy's shoulders and drew her into a hug. For a few moments, Amy allowed herself to be held before pulling away.

"Yes, I'm okay . . . It's just . . . " Involuntarily, Amy's gaze moved to the window where she could see Alex, John, and Nathaniel weeding the vegetable garden in the distance. Maybe she was being silly. Alex had been nothing but nice to her—a little intense, perhaps, but always kind.

"Amy?" Mildred asked, laying a soft hand on her arm. "Is something troubling you?"

"It's nothing." She was probably being silly. "I'm fine. Really."

"I hope that someday, you'll feel comfortable enough to tell me the truth. Go wash up. I need your help preparing the dinner for tonight."

"Me? Are you sure? I can't cook to save my life."

"Never mind that; I haven't met a hopeless case in the kitchen yet. Quickly now, wash those hands . . . "

Shaking her head, Amy ran to the bathroom and scrubbed her hands until all the mud, dust, and hay from the stalls was gone. Drying them on a fluffy, brown towel, she hurried back to the kitchen. She was just about to cross the kitchen threshold when a hand wrapped around her wrist, stopping her. He must have backtracked around from the barn to the house in time to catch her alone.

Alex stepped forward, his hand still on her wrist, pressing against the soft bandages. "Hi, Amy."

"Alex. Do you mind?" she asked, gesturing to his hand.

With a loud sigh, Alex dropped her arm.

She crossed her arms over her chest. "Is there something I can help you with?" she asked, moving closer to the doorway until Mildred was in her line of sight. Her gray head was bent over a recipe book as she measured some brown herbs and threw them into a large bowl.

"Are you okay?" Alex asked.

"Yes, I'm fine. Why?"

"That other boy—Brad. You know him?"

"Yes, Brad and I go to the same school."

"Are you friends or what?"

A sudden—and probably stupid—idea came into her mind, and the words were out of her mouth before she could think them through properly. "Actually, Brad is my ex-boyfriend." Why had she said that? She had no clue—but the idea took hold, and glancing up at Alex's dark eyes, it suddenly sounded like the best idea she'd ever had.

Alex stiffened in surprise, his brow bending into a deep frown. "I see," he said.

"Look, Alex, I think you're a great guy. I would like for us to be friends."

Bright color filled Alex's cheeks, and he ran his hand through his short hair. Had it been longer before he'd come to Heavenly Haven? "Sure, Amy. I'd like that."

Maybe this time, he would get the message. "Anyway, I'm sure you have a ton to do. I know I do." She hurried away, back into the kitchen. Mildred glanced up from her recipe book.

"All washed up?" Mildred asked. A large tray of ground beef lay on the counter before her. Beside it were bundles of peppers, onions, eggs, and breadcrumbs.

"Yes." Amy pulled an apron from the counter and slung it over her head, tying a knot at the small of her back. "What are we making?"

"Beef patties for hamburgers. First, chop the onions and peppers and add them to the ground beef and then add the eggs. After that is all combined, we add in the bread crumbs. Then comes the fun part. You don't mind getting your hands dirty, do you?"

Leaning closer, Amy poked at the mountain of ground beef, slowly rolling a thin piece between her thumb and forefinger. It was sticky and cold. "No, I think I'll be okay."

"Great! Okay, first—the onions."

Once all the onions and peppers had been chopped into small pieces and combined with the ground beef, eggs, and breadcrumbs, Amy took a handful of the mixture and flattened it into a round shape between her hands.

Mildred glanced over at her. "See, I told you. You're a natural."

A feeling of pride filled Amy's chest at her accomplishment and at Mildred's praise. "Thank you. I've never made anything like this before. Mom usually politely tells me to leave the kitchen. I think she's afraid I'll burn the house down."

"Why, did you set something on fire?"

"No, I don't think I've ever been in the kitchen long enough to do that. My mom probably just sees how useless I am in the kitchen and wants to save me from the aggravation of the experience."

Mildred was silent for a long while, as if thinking carefully about how to answer. "Often, feelings of uselessness stem from deeper feelings of guilt and shame—like hiding a deep pain behind the feeling that we can do nothing right or convincing ourselves that trying anything new is setting ourselves up for failure, so why bother?" She let the words hang in the air between them. "It might be that your mother saw how anxious it made you to be in the kitchen, and that was her way of helping you out." She mushed more of the mixture, squeezing it with practiced ease into another burger.

That was a perspective Amy hadn't thought of before. "But how do you overcome those feelings?" she asked quietly after two or three more burgers were made.

"Give it to God. Talk. Pray. Sometimes, all it takes is the simple step of believing in ourselves—believing that we matter and that it's worth the effort of trying to change for the better."

Amy swallowed back the sudden wad of emotion clogging her throat and squeezed her eyelids shut to stop her tears. Mrs. Vaughn had often spoken of the mercy and grace of God to the broken, but somehow, Amy had never thought it could possibly apply to her circumstances. After all, she'd let it happen and done nothing to stop herself from being taken advantage of. How could she possibly be worthy of grace when the very thing that had happened to her was her own fault?

"I don't know if I am strong enough to make that choice, to reach that step."

"I'm not going to sugar-coat it for you. Most people need to be shoved into that first step, but once they take it—once they take the Savior's hand and invite Him into their fight—they are never the same."

Amy cleared her throat and pulled back from her preparations. "If you don't mind, I think I need some air." It couldn't be true. God didn't love her, did He? But wouldn't it be something if He did? Amy scoffed at the ridiculous thought. She was dirty and defiled; no one could love her. And the one person who had understood her was no longer able to help her. She wanted to hope in such a love, but it was impossible. Maybe for others, but not for her.

Focusing on her task again, Mildred nodded. "Well, we need wood for the grill. Why don't you go over to the woodpile and load a few logs into the wheelbarrow? Griffin should be around soon to chop the wood into pieces we can use for the fire."

"Where is the woodpile?" Amy washed and dried her hands.

"Just beyond the vegetable garden, next to where we have the bonfire."

Amy nodded and removed the apron from around her waist. A fresh breeze blew into her face as she walked out the door. The screen slapped closed behind her. Closing her eyes, she breathed in the silence and fresh air. Her heart was heavy, her emotions confused.

Mildred didn't understand—how could she? She had never made the mistakes Amy had or lived the life Amy did. It was part of her punishment for her sins that her parents broke up. She deserved all the pain she got because she was such a terrible person—useless, pathetic and unlovable.

She trudged down the porch steps and ambled to the barn in search of a wheelbarrow. Once she'd located one on the side of the barn, she went in search of the woodpile. It was exactly where Mildred had said it would be.

Piled high against the back wall of a building were neatly packed quarter rounds of wood. Twenty feet away from the wood was the concrete circle with a low barrier used for the weekly bonfire. Pale gray ashes were all that remained from the previous night. One hundred yards from the benches at the base of a group of tall trees were round tree stumps, some small and some large. Beside them was more wood.

Sighing softly, she bent to retrieve the first block of timber, followed by another and another until the wheelbarrow all but groaned under the load. Clasping the handles with both hands, she attempted to lift the wheelbarrow and push it back to the house. It was too heavy, and her puny arms weren't up to the challenge of lugging tons of wood any distance. Accepting the inevitable, Amy began to unload the pieces of wood, returning two to the stack.

"Can I help?" Brad appeared from between the low-slung branches of the oak tree.

"Brad! I didn't see you there," Amy exclaimed.

"Sorry." He shrugged his broad shoulders, a friendly smile playing at the edges of his mouth. Why was she looking at his mouth? It was just a smile. Everyone smiled. Brad gently took her hands from the handles and replaced them with his own. "Where to?"

"Back to the main house. Mildred wants them for the barbecue later. She said Griffin will come and chop them smaller."

"Okay. Well, in that case, I guess we're heading in the same direction. Griffin asked me to see if I could find a decent branch to make a hoe handle. One of them broke, and he needs to replace it. He said to meet him at the house; there was another chore that needed doing."

"Ah. I think that might be the wood-chopping."

"Perhaps. Anyway, let's get these to the house."

Brad grinned. His smile was nice; she'd never noticed it before. Maybe it was the ridiculous lie she'd told Alex that made her suddenly notice it. She would have to tell Brad what she'd done and hope she could contain her embarrassment when he laughed at her.

Bracing for humiliation, she said, "I have something I need your help with."

"Sure. Does it have something to do with Alex?"

"It does." She shifted uncomfortably, twisting her hands together. Color bloomed hotly in her cheeks.

"Has he done something to you? You seemed very uncomfortable around him," Brad said. His tone was conversational, but she could hear the underlying tension in his voice.

"No, no. I mean, not yet. I don't know. I don't think he's getting the message that I want only to be friends."

"Good. I mean, good that he hasn't done anything." Brad rubbed an agitated hand down his face, resting the wheelbarrow on the ground. "What's the favor?"

Amy swallowed hard. "Can you pretend that we used to date?"

A myriad of emotions flashed over Brad's features. "You know dating on the farm is illegal."

"How do you know that?"

"Come on, Amy, think about it. Why would we both end up here if it wasn't some kind of rehabilitation center?"

She guessed it made sense; she was here, after all, to get help for whatever was going on with her. "Okay. But we aren't dating—we just *used* to date, and you're still protective of me. Would that work?" She shrugged, uncomfortable with the way this conversation was going.

Brad nodded. "Sounds reasonable. I can do that."

Relief, sweet and acute, fell from her shoulders. It was nice to have a friend who would help her at the farm, no matter how ridiculous the favor sounded to her own ears. Generally speaking, Brad was a nice guy. He would probably hold up his side of the bargain. As long as she didn't think too much about what had happened with Willow and Candice, everything would be fine.

"Well, now, that's settled. We'd better get these logs to the house before Griffin accuses me of slacking." He laughed, breaking the strange tension that seemed to fill the air between them.

She allowed herself a laugh. "Thank you for understanding. I was bracing myself for mad laughter and tears."

"I wouldn't do that to you." Brad slung his arm onto Amy's shoulder, just like he had earlier. "Don't worry—friends look out for friends."

CHAPTER THIRTEEN

G riffin was waiting for them when Brad and Amy came around the house, side by side. The handles of the wheelbarrow pressed into the still-open cuts on Brad's hands. His muscles felt stronger, his body healthier. It felt good to be useful, to be busy, to not sit by himself somewhere and let the guilt consume him. And it felt good for Amy to put a little faith in him.

"Ah, here you two are," Griffin said, eyeing Amy and then Brad. "Amy, you seem to have found the wood all right. Do you need help collecting more wood?"

Uncertainty flashed through Amy's eyes at Griffin's suggestion.

Brad broke in. "I think I can handle it. Amy, didn't you need to . . ." There he was coming to her aid again. Was he developing some kind of hero complex with Amy?

"Yes, I'm sure Mildred must be wondering where I've run off to. Thank you, Brad." She gazed at him thankfully.

Something moved strangely in his chest. He didn't quite know what to do with it—but it scared him to death. Heat built around his neck, and he was glad it didn't reach as far as his face. "You're welcome." He watched as Amy hurried around the porch, up the stairs, and into the house.

"Brad? You ready to get to chopping?" Griffin asked.

Brad pulled his gaze from the closed door and focused his attention on the axe extended to him from Griffin's hand. "Sure. Are you going to show me how?"

"Would you like me to?"

Brad nodded. "Please."

Griffin paused for a moment before retrieving another axe resting against the porch by the wood pile. "Help me unload these, and then we can get to work. Mildred will want to start the barbecue soon, and I won't have her going on about how I ruined her dinner." Griffin chuckled, and Brad found himself joining him.

An hour later, Brad's arms ached from the constant swinging of the axe. The blisters on his hands were bleeding from the impact of the axe meeting the wood and reverberating through his skin. This time, however, he had remembered to wear his gloves.

During the repetitive work, his mind had returned once or twice to his conversation with Amy. He and Amy had been in the same friendship group since they were freshmen with Willow, Felicia, and the rest of the guys on the football team. The beginning of their senior year had been the best—and then the worst.

Willow was still in a coma from a car accident, although he wasn't sure what had happened to her. He'd heard a rumor of some kind of conversion, but who knew? With Willow, it could also be a joke. After the fiasco with Candice, he'd bid Willow goodbye one night at a party, and he hadn't been back since. He wasn't sure he had really liked Willow—not like Candice. Candice—it always came back to her.

These thoughts made his mouth water for a drop of alcohol. He wanted to convince himself that he hadn't loved her, but the truth was, he had—and selfishly, it had not been enough to do right by her. When

Willow had presented herself as a substitute, he'd opened his arms to her, embracing an escape from his problems. "Yeah, and now you can't forgive yourself for being such an idiot," Brad muttered to himself.

"That is the first step to forgiveness: admitting responsibility."

Brad looked up from his work to see Mildred smiling serenely down at him from the porch railing. He snorted, dismissing Mildred's words. When Candice had told him of her pregnancy, he'd panicked. He wasn't old enough to be a dad, and what if he turned out to be anything like his father? His kid would end up as messed up as he was.

No, it was better he not have anything to do with the kid. But that didn't stop him from thinking of him or her. He didn't even know how far along Candice was, but seeing as they'd been together only once, he could probably figure it out. Possibly, Felicia could remind him of the date of the party. Mildred cleared her throat quietly, drawing him from his musings and returning his attention to her.

"It's never too late for forgiveness; you only have to ask. Tell me, Brad, do you think what you did was unforgivable?"

There was no doubt about that. He nodded.

Mildred nodded sagely. "I don't know your story, but only when the truth is out can healing and forgiveness take place. I hope you will find healing here, Brad."

Maybe for Amy, but not for him. He didn't know what had happened to Amy, nor why she had tried to take her own life; but if anyone deserved healing, it was she.

"I doubt it. Forgiveness isn't possible for someone like me, I assure you."

Mildred smiled kindly, and he thought she seemed a little sad. "We shall see. The Lord works in mysterious ways, and with Him, all things are possible. In Matthew 19:26, it says, '*With man, this is impossible, but with God all things are possible.*' Forgiveness is impossible for one such as yourself, but with God"—she paused, and a peaceful smile washed over the sad one—"with God, anything is possible."

Brad gripped the axe tighter, wincing as the stiff wood pressed against his ragged skin. Did he deserve forgiveness? No. Did he want it? With everything in him. But how? Maybe it was time he lay all his cards on the table and speak to Griffin.

Later that evening, as everyone sat around the bonfire enjoying the peaceful night, Brad was still wrestling with whether he should talk to Griffin. But his thoughts were interrupted when he looked up and saw Alex trying to corner Amy again.

Brad jumped up and told him in low tones to stay away from her, or there would be consequences. By the time he'd returned to sit beside her at the bonfire, Alex had stormed off into the night, followed quickly by Nathaniel and John, one of the older counselors. He hoped Alex didn't come back. Once Alex was gone, Amy relaxed and seemed to enjoy the bonfire.

"Are you okay?" he asked her.

She shivered, and without thinking, he wrapped his arm around her and pulled her into his side for warmth. "Yes, I guess. I mean, why does he do that? Haven't I been clear enough?" A single tear rolled down her cheek.

"Maybe I should speak to Griffin, or you should speak to Mildred." Brad wanted to punch Alex. Brad knew he was the last person to talk of chivalry and the right way to treat a lady, but his mother had taught him a few things before she had been taken from him.

Amy quickly shook her head. "No, I mean, what if he needs to be here, like we do? What if that's just the way he is? Maybe I'm taking his actions too personally."

Brad felt himself tense. "Amy, no. If the guy makes you uncomfortable, there must be a reason why you feel that way."

Amy's expression dropped into sadness. "Maybe I did something to encourage him."

Fire bubbled up in his veins. "No, you didn't. You deserve to be respected—even by a loser such as Alex. Everyone does."

Amy lapsed into silence. He wondered where her thoughts had gone. Wherever they'd moved to, a deep frown settled between her eyebrows, and she shivered again. He didn't think it was from the cold this time, but he held her close nonetheless, if only to assure her he was on her side and would be for as long as he she needed him.

A part of him feared he'd mess up his friendship with Amy just as he'd messed up his relationship with Candice. This time, his heart wasn't involved, though—so how could he mess it up? He would keep Alex from Amy, and that was all—he hoped.

The cottage was nearly silent when Brad found the courage to seek out Griffin. The evening had been pleasant enough after Alex had left, and he had enjoyed spending time with Amy.

"Brad? What are you doing up?" Griffin flicked on a switch, and the living room was bathed in light, bringing Brad back to the present.

"Can we talk?" he asked.

CHAPTER FOURTEEN

"I guess it's you and me again," Amy whispered to the cup of chamomile tea resting between the palms of her hands. It was warm, and the smell of flowers was comforting. The tea didn't taste all that great, but it worked wonders for calming her heart when she was sure a trip to the ER was in order. She took another sip, her thoughts wandering to Brad.

Brad was a great friend, and despite their messed-up situations, she was glad they were here together. It was surprising to see a side of him she'd only heard about from her friends. Brad was kind and chivalrous, and most of all, he was the only man she felt safe enough to reveal her thoughts to. Her father used to fill that role, but . . .

It was strange because she knew of Brad's reputation—there was no one at Bethel who didn't know what had happened between Brad, Willow, and Candice—but despite all that, he'd come to her rescue again and again tonight.

"Up again, Amy?" Mildred asked as she walked on slippered feet into the kitchen and flipped on the switch for the kettle.

Amy sighed. "Another night, another nightmare," she said, almost to herself. A small part of her hoped Mildred would hear and ask questions; the rest of her dreaded the thought.

Mildred moved around the kitchen; and soon, the warm, sweet smell of hot chocolate wafted past Amy's nose. From a wooden box on top of the large, industrial-sized fridge, Mildred withdrew a Bible and went to sit in the same seat she had been occupying two nights before when Amy had come into the kitchen after her panic attack. Mildred quietly took a sip of her hot chocolate and flipped the pages of the book. She dipped her head and closed her eyes for a few moments before returning to her reading.

Amy sipped her tea. Silence hung in the room like a snowstorm.

"Mildred," Amy said. Quivers of fear moved through her body, and she felt the beginnings of a panic attack racing her blood through her veins and pounding her heart into an unnatural rhythm. Why had she opened her mouth? She should have just stayed silent.

"Yes?" With a small, encouraging smile, Mildred tapped the seat beside her, gesturing for Amy to join her at the table. Amy rose from the bar stool beside the kitchen island and sat in the chair next to Mildred.

"Ah, nothing. Never mind." Amy sipped her tea, stalling.

Mildred sighed. "Would you like to talk?"

When Amy didn't answer, she went on. "You are safe here. I will listen, and I will not judge; it isn't my place. I want to help with whatever is troubling you, and I hope that you trust me enough to know that I won't share anything with anyone unless you ask me to. Not even your parents."

Amy nodded and placed her tea on the table, spilling some of the hot liquid between her shaking hands. She tried to take another sip, but the shaking was so severe that the tea only sloshed over the side of the mug. Mildred gently took the mug from her and placed it on the table.

"Do you want to tell me about the panic attacks?"

Amy braced her hands on either side of her mug, careful not to touch it. She drew a few deep breaths to steady herself enough to talk. "I don't know why it happens," she began, "but when I go to bed at night, I get so afraid of anything and everything. What if my parents die and leave me alone? What if Logan can't look after me? What if something happens to my friends? What if I die in a car crash; would anyone even miss me? What if I fail the math test I know I've studied for? What if my teacher suspects me of cheating, and while I know I didn't do anything, I can't prove it? What if . . . " She exhaled. She was always so afraid.

A warm, gentle hand reached out for Amy's hand, which shook on the checkered tablecloth. "Amy, you are safe. None of those things are likely to happen, but my saying so is not going to take away your anxiety over them. Do you believe something will happen to your family soon? Are they unwell? In danger?"

"Well, no, and I know that. But at night, fear consumes me, and I can't seem to convince myself that something horrible is not going to happen to those I care about. My thoughts get dark and drag to a place where I feel so helpless and useless . . . "

Mildred waited while Amy took another shaky sip of her tea and then, with more success, placed the mug on the table.

"Do you remember the first time you felt this way? Anxious, panicked?"

Amy thought back. She wasn't entirely sure, but it was sometime when she was young. In elementary school, perhaps. "I'm not sure. I do remember being in the sixth grade and waking up in the middle of the night on the floor, my heart pounding behind my ribs. I don't remember if it was because of a dream or what had happened that day—only that I was so afraid, I could barely breathe."

"How often do you experience being anxious or panicked? Daily? Weekly? Monthly?"

That one wasn't hard at all. "Almost constantly. It comes and goes, depending on how stressed I am with school, homework, my friends, and so on—and whether I can distract myself enough. As for the panic attacks, they come every night with the dreams."

Mildred nodded again and wrote something on a piece of paper Amy now saw alongside her Bible.

"Why do you think you were sent to Heavenly Haven?"

"Because I tried to take my life." Unconsciously, Amy ran her fingers down the thin bandages that covered her wrists. Mary Anne, the on-call nurse who visited the farm periodically, had checked her bandages that morning; and by the looks of things, her cuts were healing well. Mary Anne had said the stitches would come out in a couple of weeks, and Amy was grateful to hear it. She would bear the scars for the rest of her life. However, a part of her was grateful she'd failed.

"What made you try to take your own life?"

Amy shifted uncomfortably in her chair. She didn't want to think of that night—the party, the alcohol, the blood. The images she remembered were marred by tears and the frightened tones of her parents' and Logan's voices. Why had she put the glass on her wrist? Why had she tried to end her life? Was it hopelessness? Did she feel worthless, like she would never be good enough? Was it that she hated herself so much that it seemed better to take her life than live it?

Mildred sat quietly, watching while Amy puzzled her thoughts through in her mind. It was all a mix of sounds, voices, and choices that made little sense. "To get away," she finally whispered. Away from her grief, her stupidity at school, her self consciousness about her shape—and the list went on.

"Have another sip of tea," Mildred said, handing Amy the mug. Amy inhaled the floral scent of the tea and took a few sips. The cup was cooler but still warm, so she held onto it.

"What did you want to get away from?"

"My dad cheated on my mom when I was four. They patched it up and tried again, and it seemed like things were going well until I came home to find my mom had caught my dad at it again. My cousin Olivia was my best friend, but she died two summers ago in a boating accident. Things at school have been tough; I'm failing two of my four classes. One of my good friends—if she could be called that—was in a serious car accident a few months ago and is in a coma. Another friend, Candice, left school to have a baby. She and Brad had a really bad breakup. And I know I hurt her, too."

She paused. Her hands were shaking again, and beneath her skin, her heart raced like a freight train. "I want to stop being afraid and worried all the time. Sometimes, I feel so self-conscious that I think everyone is looking at me. Other times, I'm so afraid someone will see inside me and find out how messed up I am," she finally admitted. And then there was her greatest secret, the one she'd never told anyone.

Mildred stood from her chair and drew Amy into a hug. It was comforting and warm, and Mildred had a scent that was all comfort and cookies, like Amy's grandma. She led Amy by the hand over to the nearest sofa in the living room and sat beside her, still holding Amy's hand. "Why do you feel like everyone is looking at you? What would they see?"

Amy drew her hand from Mildred's and sank into the soft cushions of the sofa. Her stomach curled into a knot so tight, she felt sick. "It happened when I was young—eleven or twelve, I think. He was one of Logan's friends but a few years older. Maybe fifteen or sixteen. He would regularly come over to play video games.

"When Logan would go out for pizza or to work, he would find me. At first, I liked the attention, but then, he wanted more from me. It was months later when I found the courage to tell him to stop and that I didn't want to do anything with him. He never touched me again, and I made sure the two of us were never alone again. Two years later, he left for college. I was relieved I wouldn't have to see him anymore, but I never told anyone what had happened."

By this time, tears ran down her cheeks like torrents, the sickness at her confession swirling like muck in her stomach. But despite her shame, it felt good to tell someone.

"Logan, my brother, would have been devastated if he ever found out. And I never told my parents because what difference would it make when he wasn't around anymore? I mean, I *let* him do those things to me. Why didn't I tell him no in the first place?"

The trickle of tears turned into sobs. Her shoulders heaved up and down as she tried to control her emotions, but the tears would not be stemmed. After a moment, she stopped trying to stop her tears; and when Mildred offered her a soft shoulder, she let herself cry.

CHAPTER FIFTEEN

"I got my girlfriend pregnant, and then I left her for another woman." Brad clenched his hands into hard fists, keeping his eyes trained on the dusty, beige carpet below his feet. He balanced on the edge of the sofa, too wound up to sink into its soft embrace. Shame at his actions sat heavily on his shoulders, and he couldn't lift his head to meet Griffin's gaze.

When Griffin said nothing, he continued. "I wasn't good to her when we were together, not in the way I should have been. Candice deserved so much better." He clenched his jaw and stood, running his hand through his hair. Tension pressed so hard against his shoulders that he was sure he would feel the tearing of muscles at any moment.

He'd pushed her, and like the person she was, she'd eventually given in to his demands. At first, it felt like an outstanding victory, a high like the one he felt at the end of a football game. As time went on and Candice began to reject his demands, Willow filled that need to prove he was a man—more than the failure his father said he was.

"I hooked up with another girl and told Candice, my ex, that I didn't want her or the baby." Bile burned in his throat at his callous demand and his disregard for Candice's feelings. Guilt, like a wave on the shore, crashed into him with more force than a tsunami. He remembered her face, the devastation in Candice's eyes when he'd met her in the hallway, his hand in Willow's.

"Did she want the baby?" Griffin asked.

"I don't know. The day after, she left school and didn't come back. I got some papers in the mail a month back—something about legal rights—so I guess she didn't. Dad signed them, made me sign them, and that was it."

Griffin rested back into the sofa. "When did you start drinking?"

"Freshman year, at parties." He swallowed hard, memories flicking through his head like the reel of a movie. "I used to drink only at parties. And, you know, with the guys, to relax after games. But . . ." He trailed off.

"It got out of hand?" Griffin sighed softly. "That's how it started for me."

Brad was silent, not daring to breathe. *What? Did Griffin really understand?*

"It felt good to let go—to not have to worry about the expectations and pressures placed on a high school athlete. Do you play football?"

"Quarterback. How did you know?" Brad sank down into the soft cushions of the sofa, as if being dragged down by the brown material.

"Because I know the swagger. I used that swagger to get anything and anyone I wanted. I abused the power I held as captain of the football team. My team needed me; the coaches needed me; and so . . ." Griffin wove his hand between his knees and leaned forward. "I did what anyone in my position would do; I took advantage of it. I didn't care who I hurt, only that whatever I did or whomever I hooked up with made me feel better. I thought I was invincible and that nothing could touch me."

Brad swallowed hard. Griffin's story sounded so much like his own.

"Are you going to college?" Griffin asked.

"Yeah, I'm supposed to go in the fall. Full scholarship to Alabama."

"Do you think you will?"

"Maybe a week ago, I would have said definitely, but now, I'm not so sure. Who wants a drunk on their team?"

Griffin was silent for a long moment, nodding quietly to himself. "Why do you think you are here, Brad?"

Brad rubbed the back of his neck and peered at a small, round stain on the carpet. "DUI in the town square in my hometown. My dad knows the mayor and managed to keep me out of jail. He sent me here instead."

"Sounds like he cares a lot about you."

Brad snorted. "The only thing Adrian Thorn cares about is his image, his company, and his money. I'm the embarrassment, the thing he tries to hide—a blot on his perfect image." The last words delivered themselves hoarsely from his rapidly closing throat. He'd learned to control his anger; instead of letting it out, where it would destroy things, he held it in till the noose of rage was so tight around his neck, he could barely breathe.

"What about your mom? Where is she?"

As quickly as the anger had come, it was rushed out by grief. Pain knifed his chest, and a few errant drops ran down his cheeks. He wiped at them with his fingers. "She died. Cancer. I was a freshman."

Griffin knitted his hands between his knees. "Do you think that was the real reason you started drinking?"

If Brad thought about it, Griffin was most likely right. He always told himself it was to relax, to hide, to be one of the guys. But really, he probably drank because he was hurting. He had just lost his mother, and he couldn't live up to the expectations of his father. He had desperately needed a place to belong.

"Probably." He shrugged. "Does it matter?"

"When dealing with an addiction, Brad, it's important to find the source to know why you are looking to your vice—in this case, alcohol—instead of dealing with the situation you want to hide from."

Griffin walked to a small fridge on the wall of the living room. The cottage didn't have a kitchen, and they ate all their meals at the main farmhouse; but it had a fridge for beverages—water, pop, and fruit juice for the guys who stayed there. He retrieved a bottle of water and tipped it in Brad's direction. Brad nodded and caught the bottle as it launched across the room toward him.

"How do you feel about the situation with Candice?"

Brad cracked open the bottle's lid and took a long swallow. The water slid down his throat, cooling the fiery ring he'd felt when this discussion with Griffin had begun. "I should have done better by her, not taken up with Willow. I don't know. All I know is that this guilt is chewing a hole in my gut, and I can't seem to get rid of it. Drinking helped, you know? It helped control the feelings. Numbed them so I wouldn't feel them." He sighed. "I sound like such a loser."

Griffin chuckled. "'Boys don't cry'?"

Brad nodded.

"It's a lie, you know. Men do cry; they need to. How do you deal with an emotion if you don't feel you can express it? Crying is cleansing—like catharsis for the soul. It doesn't make you less of a man to admit you are weak. You become less when you are unable to admit you are struggling to deal with hurt, grief, expectation, and yes, even guilt." Griffin took a swig from his own bottle and replaced the cap.

"I guess I feel like I should say I'm sorry and find out what's going on with the baby—see how they're both doing. She probably never wants to see me again, and with the papers signed, she doesn't need to. But a few months from now, there is going to be a little boy or girl, and I'll spend the rest of my life thinking, *What if?*"

"Do you know if the baby is being adopted or if she has decided to keep it?"

"No, she never said. I haven't seen or spoken to her since that day." He paced the stretch of the room again. "I haven't really tried to, either."

"Brad, if you feel that talking to Candice will bring you closure, then I think it would be worth it to try to find her and have a conversation."

"What if she doesn't want to see me?"

"Then at least you'll know you tried. I think we should pray about it."

Brad didn't want to—prayer had not helped when his mother had passed—but there in that room, he was willing to let Griffin try. Griffin bowed his head, and Brad did the same, allowing Griffin's soft pleas for comfort and guidance to wash over him.

"Amen." Griffin stood and cuffed Brad on the shoulder. "I think we should try to get some sleep," he said, checking his watch, "for what remains of the night. The sun will be up long before I'm ready for it."

Brad glanced at the clock on the wall. It was late, and sunrise was only a few hours away. His eyes felt like they were filled with sand. Although his body wept from exhaustion, the soul-sucking weight in his chest felt lighter. He pushed open the door of his room and quickly got ready for bed. The book Griffin had given him still lay exactly where he'd left it on his first day at the ranch. He picked it up, flipping through the pages with his fingers. The soft, leafy pages were a creamy color. Small, black-printed words were written in two columns on the pages. Brad stopped flipping and opened the book, laying it on his knees, where he saw Matthew 11:28: "Come to me, all you who are weary and burdened, and I will give you rest."

It wasn't only his body that was tired. He felt world-weary and old, like someone who'd lived much longer than seventeen years. He could use a rest. He closed the book, laid it gently back onto the table, and crawled into bed, pulling the cover over his head and blocking out the full moon.

Maybe someday, he would find rest. He closed his eyes and tried hard to remember his mother—her gentle voice, her smile when he spoke to her, her scent. He missed her terribly.

Then his thoughts turned to Candice. He would find her, somehow, if only to say how sorry he was and to find out about the baby. Maybe then he would be able to let go of their combined past, and the guilt would leave him. As sleep slowly took over, he realized something: in the hours after dinner, he hadn't thought about a drink once.

CHAPTER SIXTEEN

Things sure did look different in the morning. Amy stretched, yawning loudly, before climbing out of bed. Instead of feeling an acute sense of relief at telling Mildred about her pain, unease climbed up her spine.

Trying her best to dismiss the self-conscious pounding of her heart, she showered, dressed, and followed her nose down the stairs to the welcoming smell of coffee and frying bacon. She paused outside the kitchen as a glimpse of a person pacing the porch caught her eye. She slipped on her shoes and walked out into the fresh morning air, where the figure swung around. She found herself staring into the fatigue-lined face of Brad.

"Are you okay?" she asked him.

He smiled and shrugged. He looked unsure and a little uncomfortable at seeing her. Maybe it was because of their conversation the day before.

"Morning, Amy. I'm okay, but I didn't get much sleep last night."

"You and me both," she said, moving closer.

The sound of work boots thumping over the wooden slats of the porch rose behind them, and she was suddenly pulled to Brad's chest, his arm resting low on her back.

"It's Alex," Brad whispered.

Amy nodded and threw her arms around Brad's back, hugging him close. Brad's arms tightened around her and held on, even when she was sure the necessity had passed. The cool tip of his nose brushed against the sensitive skin of her ear, and she did her best to suppress a shiver.

As if sensing her discomfort, he roughly cleared his throat and took a step back. "Sorry, he hung around for a bit. Just wanted to make sure he got it."

"That's okay; no harm done. Are you ready for breakfast? Mildred mentioned last night that we're expected to go to church with her and the other counselors this morning."

Brad frowned and crossed his arms over his chest. "I didn't sign up for that."

"I don't think you get to sign up; you're kinda just told to go."

Brad's stiff shoulders relaxed a tad as his arms came back in line with his body. "Yeah, I guess."

Griffin opened wide the screen door, and the most wonderful smell of pancakes and syrup wafted outside, making her stomach growl.

"You guys comin'? Time's a-wastin'," he said, before stepping back inside.

"Let's get some breakfast," Amy said.

She reached out for Brad's hand and tugged him with her into the house. His hand was warm and dry, with small calluses that she knew came from his intimate knowledge of a football. It was only when they'd reached the doorway to the kitchen that Brad let go. If she didn't know better, she would think he seemed reluctant to release her hand.

She glanced up and found Brad looking down at her, the most peculiar expression on his face, before he blinked and looked at the bustling around them. Tingles still danced across the sensitive pads of her fingers; and even though she knew tingles usually meant a panic attack was on its way, she was sure they were there now for another reason—one she didn't want to look at too closely.

"Ah, Amy and I thought we saw Brad skulking outside on the porch. Good morning," Mildred said, with her usual flamboyance. "I hope you're hungry—it seems I was a bit overzealous with the pancakes this morning."

Brad smiled, and Amy felt a little hitch in her stomach. "Yes, ma'am," he said. "I'm starving."

"Yeah, starving for something," Alex muttered behind Amy. Amy stiffened, and she felt Brad go rigid beside her. She turned and glared at Alex, whose gaze jumped defiantly between Amy and Brad. Brad said nothing, but the way he was working his jaw warned that he didn't appreciate Alex's comment.

"Is there a problem, boys?" Griffin asked, muscling his way between the two.

Brad dropped his gaze at the same time Alex did. "No, Griffin," they said together.

Mildred, seemingly oblivious, beamed. "That's what I like to hear—a good, healthy appetite."

Amy brushed her hand against Brad's to let him know she appreciated him standing up for her. Brad's mouth curved infinitesimally, and she felt him touch her hand in acknowledgement. Alex glared one last time at the two of them as Griffin moved away, spinning on his heel and stalking off to where Nathaniel held a plate laden with pancakes. The two whispered to each other, and then, when Alex's plate was full, they disappeared into the early sunlight to eat on the porch.

Brad tipped his head to the living room, and Amy nodded in return.

"That was unpleasant," Brad said in a low voice.

"Yeah, good thing Griffin showed up."

Brad nodded, his expression troubled. "I may be mistaken, but I think if that guy got half a chance to beat me up, he would take it."

"I think he's just jealous."

"Let's hope so."

"Everything all right?" Griffin asked, coming to stand beside them. His gaze traveled from Brad to Amy and then to Brad again. "Is there something I need to know about you and Alex?"

Brad straightened. "I think it's a territory issue."

"Territory?" Griffin's gaze swept to Amy. "Do I need to intervene?"

"No intervention necessary," Brad said, casually sliding his hands into the front pockets of his black jeans.

"Good. You two had better get to the kitchen. We leave for church in thirty minutes, and Mildred does not allow anyone to be late."

Amy followed Brad and Griffin back and quickly filled her plate with two golden brown pancakes, a few strawberries, and a cup of coffee with two sugars and cream. She took her place beside Bethany and was surprised to feel the brush of Brad's shoulder as he settled beside her. Determined not to give the others any more to talk about, she turned to the girl on her right.

"Hi, Bethany, how are you today?"

Bethany was so shy, it was painful. The two girls' rooms were side by side at the top of the stairs, and there were many nights she'd heard Bethany run for the bathroom and noisily lose whatever was in her stomach. An eating disorder, she assumed.

"Okay, I guess," Bethany said before ducking her gaze back to her plate. The girl ate like a bird and was painfully thin. Amy hoped that whatever Mildred and the others were doing to help her would work because it hurt her to watch Bethany struggle to get down the little food she had on her plate.

It certainly put her own weight issues into perspective. She'd always considered herself overweight and had tried every diet there was to try. Sometimes, she'd exercised herself until she couldn't stand, and then she'd be sore for days afterward. But watching Bethany force herself to swallow and remembering the sound she'd heard the night before made her think that she didn't have it all that bad.

Bethany's green eyes rose again to Amy's. "And you?" Her gaze swiveled to Alex and Nathaniel on the porch and then to Brad.

"I'm good, thanks," Amy answered.

Bethany nodded but kept her eyes on Brad. Her expression changed from shyness to appreciation. It felt like a hot coal had been dropped into the knot inside Amy's stomach. *What on earth?* Forcing herself to smile at Bethany, she shoveled more of the fluffy pancakes into her mouth. Brad glanced at Bethany and gave her a friendly smile. Bethany's cheeks suddenly filled with color, and she became very interested in the last slice of strawberry on her plate.

"Amy, you about ready to go?" Brad asked. His gaze swept over Bethany but quickly returned to Amy.

Amy scooped up the last of her strawberries and shoved them in her mouth before finishing her coffee.

"Yeah, I'm good. Did you have enough?"

Brad nodded, but his mouth formed a hard line as his gaze slid over to Alex and Nathaniel, glaring at them from the doorway. "I lost my appetite."

Amy's gaze followed his, and she swallowed hard. "Okay, give me a minute to get my purse, and I'll meet you at the van."

"How about I just wait in the living room, and we'll go together? I don't trust those two."

She fidgeted with her plate and cutlery before going to dump them in the sink. They left the eating area together, and true to his word, Brad awaited her at the bottom of the farmhouse stairs when she came from her room. He pushed open the door, and with a gentle hand at the small of her back, he guided her down to where the van waited.

It was a tight squeeze—Brad's broad shoulders pressed into hers while Bethany sat stock-still beside her, staring at her hands for the duration of the trip. Amy rested her hand on her knee, and Brad did the same, his fingers millimeters from hers.

His warmth pressed into her was nice, safe—unlike the hairs that stood up at the back of her neck when she heard the distinct voices of Alex and Nathaniel whispering in the row behind her. Her heart seized, and her hands began to shake. Without hesitation, Brad gently linked his pinkie with hers, the way Logan always had when he wanted her to know he was with her and would protect her. She didn't know why Brad had done it; maybe it was because anxiety was leaking from every pore of her body. Gradually, her heart slowed, and the tension radiating through her relaxed. She glanced up. Brad smiled down at her, his gaze tender.

CHAPTER SEVENTEEN

"What did you think of the service?" Griffin asked Brad the following Monday.

They worked along a winding row of carrot plants at the heart of the vegetable field. Amy, Nathaniel, Bethany, and Mildred worked beside them in between a patch of tomatoes and beans. Brad gripped the hoe closer, turning the soil and bending to pull out the weeds. He threw them into a nearby sack and began to break more soil.

"It was okay, I guess. I don't get what he meant about forgiveness, though."

"Oh? Tell me what you mean."

"Well, if God loved us so much, why would He tell us to forgive those who hurt us? I mean, surely there should be an element of payback. Doesn't the Bible say something about an eye for an eye?"

Griffin's eyes sparkled with amusement. "Yes, it does—but there are two elements to forgiveness. According to Deuteronomy 32:35, God says, 'It is mine to avenge; I will repay.' But think about if the law of 'an eye for an eye' still applied. Would you like to suffer the same kind of hurt and humiliation that you gave your ex- girlfriend?" He paused and plunged his garden fork into the soil, loosening the earth around it. "And would you like for Candice to carry the feelings of guilt that *you* carry?"

"I wouldn't want that for Candice, and not a day has passed that I haven't wished I had acted differently or ended things with her on a better note."

"So, if Candice suffered from the same guilt that you bear—knowing what you do about the feeling—wouldn't you want to forgive her, if only to ease her burden?"

Brad rested his shoulder on the top of the hoe. "Yes."

"And knowing Candice like you do, do you think that she would want you to carry this heavy weight? Especially if there was an easier and lighter way, such as granting forgiveness?"

Candice *was* a great person; she was loving and forgiving, and she'd accepted so much about him. He rubbed the sweaty hair under his cap. He could see where Griffin was going with this. But it still sounded too simple.

Griffin plunged the fork into the ground again. "Forgiveness is as much for you as it is for the person who has hurt you or been hurt by you. By not asking Candice for forgiveness, you are taking the opportunity for her to have closure and for yourself to have peace in accepting it—and allowing God to do the rest."

"But I don't deserve for her to forgive me."

Griffin placed the fork on the overturned earth and dropped his gloves to the ground. He laid his hand on Brad's shoulder. "No one *deserves* forgiveness. It's not about what we deserve, it's about God's love for us and the grace He's extended to us. You don't deserve forgiveness for what you did, but the thing is that God is still willing to give it to you, irrespectively. That's the beauty of grace."

It still sounded way too simple to him. But as the hours drew on, the thought would not leave him. It was a persistent fly buzzing around his head. What if he took Griffin's advice and went to speak to Candice to ask for her forgiveness? Would he finally be able to forgive himself for being such a jerk to her?

"Hey, you coming in for lunch?" Amy asked, handing him a bottle of water. She looked adorable in her dusty Mets cap, well-worn jeans, and a faded checkered shirt she'd borrowed from Mildred.

He swiped the baseball cap from his head and emptied half the bottle over himself, shaking the droplets free as Amy squealed beside him. Laughing, he swallowed the remainder of the water and then held out his hand for another. Amy handed one over, splashing some of the water in his face as she did.

"Payback," she said with a low giggle.

Her smile stopped any thought of retaliation, and he once again questioned his sanity. Amy made him feel things he shouldn't be feeling—not when he was dealing with so much.

"Shall we?" he asked, stuffing the gloves in his back pocket and slinging the hoe over his shoulder en route back to the shed, using his other hand to try to turn Amy back toward the house. She laughed and followed him, anyway. It was becoming easier to touch her, to be around her. They weren't flagrant about their friendship, but the others knew well enough that they were close. Alex seemed to have accepted the closeness between them as the result of a past relationship, and he thankfully left Amy alone most of the time.

"Are you looking forward to your brush with freedom this weekend?" he asked as he caught up with her after returning the hoe. It was hot, and he could only imagine how much hotter it was at Heavenly Haven when summer came. He'd become accustomed to the silence of the farm and the usual sounds of horses, birds, and other wildlife. It was a pleasant change from his regular life. He wondered if Amy felt the same.

"I don't know," Amy responded. "I mean, it's so simple here, and I feel like I really am beginning to understand why I made my decision that night—but I worry about going back. What happens if I haven't learned enough, or I don't remember what I have learned? What happens if I get into a fight with my mom and everything goes to pot again?"

A slight frown bent Brad's brow as he considered her. "I suppose we won't know how to handle any situation until we've faced it and made the right choice."

"But what if I make the wrong one? I know I'm going to have to go back to school at some point, and who knows what I'm going to do about my mom? How is she going to react to my being home again? Is she going to fuss and be worried or stay on my case all the time? And Logan . . . " She groaned. "I can only imagine what he's going to do."

"It's the middle of the semester, Amy. He'll probably be at school."

"You're right. Well, what about you?"

Brad stretched his arms above his head, but quickly lowered them when he saw Amy staring at his abdominal muscles. He pulled his shirt down, grinning as he noticed the pink rising to her cheeks. "I guess my questions are a lot like yours. My dad will probably be too busy for me. So, as long as I keep my head down and don't make waves, I doubt he'll even bat an eye."

"That's sad, you know that?" She smiled impishly as Brad glanced down at her in surprise. She had rather nice lips. The moment lengthened. Suddenly, she cleared her throat, breaking the spell. "If it helps in any way, you are welcome to come and lay low at my house anytime."

Brad grew more serious. "Thank you, Amy. That means a lot."

"Yes, well, someone needs to keep an eye on you." A furious blush filling her cheeks, she said, "Now, I think we need to get to lunch before it happens without us."

Brad dragged her from the shed, laughing, as they ran hand in hand back to the farmhouse.

The barn was quiet at this time of night, but Amy didn't mind it. She couldn't sleep, despite her numerous discussions with Mildred over the last two weeks. One thing still seemed irreparably broken: her body's ability to get a good night's sleep. She shivered and lifted her hoodie over her head, slipping her hands into the pockets of her sweatpants and entering the warmth of the barn. The musty smell of horses, hay, and wood filled her senses.

Her eyes were slow to adjust to the dim light, but a quick flick of a switch bathed the stalls in light. There was something soothing about horses, she'd learned.

"Hey, Buttercup," she said, rubbing the long, black head of the mare closest to her. Johnny K., Danny, and Silverwind stuck their heads out of their stalls at the sound of her voice. She stroked Buttercup one more time before moving onto the rest.

Her dreams tonight hadn't been filled with frightening scenes of chaos—instead, the faces of her parents, Logan, and *him* appeared in array, chasing her from sleep. Maybe she would never get into the habit of sleeping, although the nightly panic attacks seemed to be getting better. She could bet they would make a reappearance this week as their weekend back home came closer and closer.

The sound of a door slamming ripped her from her reverie. Her heart sank as Alex rounded the corner of the barn door and entered the dim interior.

"I thought I would find you here," Alex said, coming toward her. His expression was innocent enough, as if their meeting was a happy coincidence; but from the predatory light burning in his brown eyes, it wasn't.

"Ah, Alex. Hi. I couldn't sleep, but I feel really tired now, so I should probably go."

"What's the hurry?" he asked, reducing the space between them to a few feet.

Her body froze, and she blinked rapidly. What was he doing here? Why had he followed her? Did anyone know he was out of his bunk? She stepped back until her back slammed into one of the barn walls.

"Look, Amy, I just want to talk," he said. Only three feet remained between them. "I can't seem to get anywhere near you with your watchdog at your side. Honestly, I just want you to give us a shot. I mean, I know you and Brad are close, but he isn't your boyfriend, so I figure . . ."

Instead of the vulnerability she would expect to find in his expression after such a plea, his face was devoid of emotion, his eyes calculating.

"And I already told you, Brad is my friend, and I am not interested in another relationship at this moment. Now, please move out of the way so that I can leave." She crossed her arms across her chest, forcing her shaking hands to still.

Alex frowned and ran his hand through his hair. "Amy." Less than three feet. She bit hard on her lip, suppressing a scream, and then there were only inches between them.

In a flurry of motion, he was out of her sight. She heard the sickening thud of flesh on flesh as Brad laid Alex flat on the floor with a practiced swing of his fist. Then she was in Brad's arms, his chest heaving against her. "Did he hurt you?"

"No, I'm okay." Aside from the terror leeching energy from her body.

A crash came; and suddenly, the entire barn, hayloft, and shed were all bathed in bright light. John, Griffin, and a few other ranchhands filled the doorway. Griffin glanced from Brad and Amy to Alex, laid out and groaning on the barn floor.

"Would someone like to tell me what is going on here?"

CHAPTER EIGHTEEN

"Here at Heavenly Haven, we have very strict rules against violence. Now, before I ask both of you to pack up your things and leave, explain to me what happened in the stable last night between the three of you," Griffin said.

He sat behind a wide, oak writing desk. It was strange to see him in this environment, shelves filled with books lining the walls around him. Close to the desk, three comfortable-looking chairs in various shades of blacks and browns stood in a circle around a stout pine coffee table with a glass top. A round rug covered the laminated floor.

Brad rubbed his tired eyes. He was exhausted; sleep had been in little supply over the last few hours. After the scene in the stable, Amy hadn't left his side. It had taken Mildred, three cups of chamomile tea, and the promise that he wouldn't kill Alex should the opportunity arise to get Amy to leave his side and go back to bed. That was sometime around three a.m.

He still didn't understand what had driven him to the stable at one in the morning, but something had jolted him awake from dreams of something terrible happening to Amy. He'd barely had time to grab a shirt before he was running toward the farmhouse on impulse. Halfway there, he'd seen the light on in the barn, and an instinct had told him she was there. He released a breath. Thankfully, he'd come in time.

"I didn't mean to scare her. I only wanted to talk," Alex said. His nose was swollen purple, bruises forming around his forehead and down his left cheek where Brad's fist had landed. "I would never hurt Amy."

Red bled over Brad's eyes, and he wondered what would happen if he hit Alex again simply for lying and trying to cover his own rear. "I don't believe you," he muttered.

Griffin raised his eyebrow at Brad. "And please tell me why, Brad."

"I think that had better be a conversation without Alex." He tangled his hands between his knees, watching the conflicting emotions racing over Griffin's face.

"Very well. Alex, you will wait for me in the sitting room while I speak to Brad. Don't move from the chair outside, or you will be sent home today."

Alex glared at Brad. "No matter what he says, I would never hurt Amy. And I never meant to scare her; I just wanted to talk to her without her watchdog."

Brad rose, and his body tensed, his fists ready. Alex held his hands up before him in a sign of surrender and left the room, slamming the door of Griffin's office closed behind him.

"Now, Brad, why do you believe Alex was going to hurt Amy last night?"

Brad drew a deep breath. "A week ago, Amy told me that Alex scared her. She said she had a feeling that he was up to no good. Although I have no proof of this, I know Amy well enough to know she wouldn't make up something like this."

"Be that as it may, your actions last night—as heroic as they might have been—are not the way conflict is handled here at Heavenly Haven. I do not expect you to apologize or even become friends with

Alex from this point on. I do, however, expect you to handle yourself in a way that is honorable and befitting someone your age. You are old enough to know that violence rarely solves anything, and this case is no different.

"I am aware that there is a history between you and Amy, but you must not let it interfere with your reasons for being at Heavenly Haven. According to our rules, this is your first warning. Any more incidents and we will have to ask you to leave Heavenly Haven, whether your treatment is complete or not. Do you understand what I am asking you?"

Brad nodded. He would have to keep a careful eye on Alex and make sure Amy remained safe without Griffin becoming too aware that there was no history between him and Amy—of the romantic nature, at least. Although, his feelings for her were rapidly heading in that direction. "I understand, Griffin." He stood and walked to the door; and as he took the handle to crack the lock, he looked over his shoulder. "Thanks for not kicking me out. I'll keep my head."

A smile brightened Griffin's firm expression. "See that you do. And you're welcome."

Brad opened the door with a nod and let himself out. He stared straight into the fire spitting from Alex's eyes, meeting them levelly. There was a challenge there.

"Alex," Griffin called, "please come in."

As Alex entered the office, Brad went in search of Amy. He found her in the laundry room with Mildred, sorting through the sheets and clothes of the people at the farm. Mildred opened the washer, showing Amy how to sort and how much soap and softener to put in a load. Amy laughed at something Mildred said, and he leaned against the doorframe, watching her. Feelings he never thought he would feel again beat inside his heart. He was falling for his friend, and he was scared to death that history would repeat itself.

"Ah, Brad, did Griffin send you to give us a hand?" Mildred asked.

Brad straightened, his gaze still fixed on Amy. She looked tired, dark rings under her eyes. Her hands trembled as she took the sheets from Mildred and tossed them into the open washer.

"No, I came to check on Amy. Would it be possible for her to take a small break?"

Mildred glanced over at Amy and said something too low for Brad to hear. Amy nodded, and Mildred drew her into a big hug. "Five minutes."

Brad nodded—at least they would have that. Amy followed Brad from the laundry room through the kitchen and out into the morning sunlight. The air smelled fresh with a hint of horses, manure, and fertilizer. Quiet as a mouse, Amy came to stand beside him. He lifted his arm and slowly wrapped it around her shoulders, drawing her into his side. For a long moment, they stood there, enjoying the silence.

"Thank you," Amy said, "for helping me last night. I don't know . . . " She turned her face into his shoulder, and he held her close, stroking his fingers up and down her back. It felt good to be strong for someone, to have Amy trust him to catch her if she fell. Maybe in its own strange way, this was how he would be able to make up for all the pain and sadness he'd caused Candice—by making sure he did not repeat his mistakes with Amy. Maybe.

She pulled back, and he tilted her chin up until their eyes met. "You are very welcome, Amy. Anytime you need me, I will be there." He meant it, to the core of his being. Fear melted from her fathomless blue eyes as they warmed, and he had the overwhelming urge to kiss her. It would be the worst thing he could do in that moment, though. So, drawing on the little self-control he possessed, he removed his arms from around her, creating space between them.

He wasn't sure if five minutes had passed, but he needed to get away from Amy before he did something really stupid. "I think our time is up."

Amy chuckled and looked up at the sky. "I can hear Mildred humming in tune with the washer. I'd better join her. Who would want to miss out on what is sure to be a riveting lesson on folding towels?"

Brad chuckled. "Hey, it beats what I'm about to do. Griffin, John, and the rest of us guys are fertilizing the fields today. Man, by the end of today, I'm likely to smell like the back of a long-horned bull." He grimaced dramatically, and Amy laughed. He loved the way she laughed. It was like a thousand happy bells ringing through the air.

"Amy," Mildred called from inside the house, "the load is done. Time to fold the towels."

"That's my cue," Amy said softly.

"And I better change and get to the field." Brad shoved his hands into his pockets to stop himself from hugging her again. She looked like she needed one, though.

"I'll see you at lunch?"

"Yeah, I'll see you then."

"Are you still going home for the weekend after that incident with Alex?"

"Yeah, but I will need to be on my best behavior from now on, or I'm finished here."

"Let's hope Alex can keep himself in check."

"I wouldn't worry about that too much."

"Oh, please tell me you didn't do anything to get into more trouble!"

"No, I think Alex and I understand each other better now." At least, he hoped that was the case.

The rest of the week flew by. Thankfully, Alex kept his distance from Amy, allowing Brad to concentrate on his duties.

Each night, Griffin and Brad would meet in the small living room of the cottage, and Griffin would ask him about his mother and father. They talked about the Bible, Griffin's past, and anything else Brad had on his mind. But during the night hours, he still saw Candice's face questioning him in his dreams, and the guilt would return.

Before he was ready, he was waving Amy away from Heavenly Haven for the weekend with a small measure of peace, knowing that they would be returning to the same hometown.

CHAPTER NINETEEN

"And here we are," Amy's mother said as she brought the car to a halt outside their family bungalow. Amy released a pent-up breath, thankful to be home but also somewhat apprehensive. Her phone felt strange in her pocket, and she pressed her hand against the side of her jeans, adjusting the foreign object.

"Do you need a minute?" her mother asked.

Amy smiled—at least, she hoped it was a smile—and shook her head. "No, I'm happy to be here."

Her mother paused before climbing from the car, closing the door behind her. She waited on the porch for a moment before turning back and gesturing for Amy to join her. Amy swung the car door open, feeling a bit like a stranger returning to a land she should remember.

A frown dipped her forehead as she recalled the circumstances of her departure. She hadn't seen the inside of her house since that night that everything had come to a head. She'd gone straight from the hospital to the ranch.

She pushed back her shoulders and remembered she didn't have anything to fear. The past was behind her, and she was working toward getting better. A visit home would not derail that. Retrieving her bag and slinging it over her shoulder, she followed her mother, who climbed the porch steps and swung open the front door.

At first, Amy didn't compute the sight that greeted her. Her father, arms spread wide open, smiled in welcome.

"Hi, honey," he said, stepping forward and drawing her into a firm hug. She sank into him, relishing the safety of her father's arms and the warm and comfort his embrace brought to her. He must have been visiting for the day to welcome her; that was the only reason her mother would allow him inside the house.

"Hi, Dad," she said, allowing her duffel bag to drop to the floor pressing back from his embrace.

"It's good to see you," he said as he stepped back, giving her space to look up into his warm, brown eyes.

"It's good to see you, too, Dad. How have you been?"

Her father glanced at her mother, and there was silence for a moment. The two seemed to be in non-verbal communication about something, but what was it?

"I've been well, thank you. Why don't you come into the kitchen? I am sure your mother has cake and something to drink."

A tingle of uncertainty crept up her spine. She studied her parents as they moved around the kitchen with practiced ease. What had she missed? Where was the animosity that had existed between them the last time she'd seen them together? Were they trying for her sake to be decent to each other—or was it more than that? Had something happened in the past two weeks?

"Mom, can I talk to you for a minute?" Amy asked. She stepped toward the doorway that led back to the living room.

"Sure, honey." Amy's mother placed the coffee mugs on the table and glanced at her father before following Amy from the room.

"What is going on?" Amy asked in a low voice. "What is he doing here?"

Her mother swallowed, and a deep crimson stained her cheeks. She shifted from one foot to the other, wringing her hands.

"When you . . . " Her mother shuddered. "When you were in the hospital, your father and I decided to . . . " Her words stuttered to a halt as she looked past Amy's shoulder and nodded.

"Your mother and I decided we needed each other after that horrible night." Amy's father choked up on the words as she turned to face him. Tears ran down his face, and he reached for her with one hand and her mother with the other, drawing them both into his chest.

"I made a mistake, Amy, but I love you and your mother and brother so much. That night in the hospital, I realized I needed to do something. I needed to change. So that night, I begged your mom for forgiveness."

Tears ran down the side of her mother's face as he sighed. "We've been seeing a pastor at Bethel Baptist Church three nights a week to try and make it work."

A sob came from her mother, and Amy felt her shoulders shake. "I'm so sorry, honey, so sorry."

Amy wanted to be mad at her father. She wanted to run and shout and scream at her mother for being so stupid, but during her time at Heavenly Haven, she'd come to understand more about forgiveness. Her father's guilt was not her own, and Amy's mother's decisions weren't hers to make. They all had to make their choices and live with them. She understood—a little, at least. Instead of giving in to the impulse to be angry, she tried to understand how the attempt she'd made to end her life had affected her family. It took a moment, but then her tears joined those of her parents.

Discussion and anger could wait for tomorrow. Today, she would allow her parents to comfort her and be a comfort in return.

The BMW's tires moved quietly over the gravel driveway of Brad's home, leaving him alone with his thoughts. He waved to the driver, although Ira was probably too far away to see the gesture. Where was his father? Would he find him inside? Brad had sent a message two days ago to expect him today; but on his release, instead of his father waiting outside the cottage at Heavenly Haven, only Ira and his father's black BMW awaited him.

He pushed down his resentment, surprised at how easily it sprang to life again, being at home. He'd worked hard to let go of the anger he carried for his father, and he thought he'd succeeded in trying to see him in a better light. Despite his hard work, it still hurt that his father could not take the time to pick him up.

He scrubbed the back of his neck, taking a moment to appreciate what he had. Brad studied his home with new eyes, ones that could see past the resentment of his father's money and status to his blessings. The house was enormous and far too large for one man and his only son—although, they did have a plethora of staff. The house itself was beautiful with two geometrically shaped stories of glistening white stacks and columns; elegant, square windows trimmed with black; and a balcony which protruded from the top floor and came to an end overlooking the shimmering blue waters of the round pool.

He hooked his backpack over his shoulder and walked, loose-limbed, toward the door. The dread that accompanied such an action in the past was gone, and only anticipation and the expectation of something better remained. He turned his key in the lock and entered his home. He stopped and looked around, breathing in the familiar smells, but there was no sound or movement. The house was impeccably clean—the way the housekeeper, Mrs. McCleary, always liked it.

Brad hadn't really expected his father to be home, but he had hoped to be wrong. Clearly, it was just another day for Adrian Thorn, even if it was an important one to Brad. Did he dare step out and call his father? Ask him something he never had—to come home, to hang out, to talk like they used to before his mother had died?

Leaving the thought hanging there for the moment, he made his way to his room and threw his bag onto his bed. Everything was neat as a pin, as always. *Thanks, Mrs. McCleary.*

He sat on the edge of the bed and gazed around the room, feeling like a stranger in his own space. In prime position stood his TV, with the gaming system neatly laid out for his use and a pile of games waiting beside it. He stood and bent to look at them. They didn't hold his interest for very long.

Sighing, he stood up, glancing at the rows and rows of trophies on his cabinet. They, too, failed to intrigue him. He was restless, uncomfortable—maybe he should do a few laps in the pool. That always used to calm his mind. His phone vibrated in his pocket then, and after two weeks without the instrument, it felt strange. He took it out to see who had messaged him. Along with the message to his father announcing his visit, he had put in a text to his friend group, too.

Hey, dude, you alive?

The message was from Jace.

Yeah, he texted back.

Want to hang out? Felicia's throwing another bash tomorrow.

Brad stared at the screen, waiting to feel some excitement at the prospect of another party and seeing his friends. But there wasn't much—or at least, there was much less than there normally would have been. Why was that? Leaving the message unanswered, he flipped through his contacts until he found Amy's number. It was going to be strange not seeing her every day. He hadn't realized how much he would miss her until the limo had turned the corner and left Heavenly Haven in a swirl of dust.

Are you home? It's Brad. I just wanted to find out if you got home safe.

Yeah, that sounded kind, concerned, and friendly, right? He thought back to the times he and Amy had spent together on the ranch. He had enjoyed their time together; even though both of them were each going through something huge, they were there for one another. Whenever he needed someone to talk to or joke with or just sit next to at meals, it was always Amy. She made him feel . . .

Brad paused as the phone in his hand buzzed. *She made me feel . . .*

Amy was the only other woman to make him feel an emotion that wasn't based on physical gratification. With her quiet laughs, her huge blue eyes, and the way she understood him even when he couldn't express himself with words . . . He liked her. As more than just a friend. He smiled and shook his head. His timing stank, but nonetheless, there it was. At least, they were friends.

The phone dropped to the floor, and he bent quickly to retrieve it. The screen was dark, and he swiped it back to life.

Amy. *Yeah, just got back. You?*

Me, too. How was the drive?

Because that didn't sound stupid at all. He just needed to know she was okay—and if he was being honest, he just wanted to hear from her. It would be too much to call her, but for now, he would be happy with a text.

It was okay. Mom was very quiet. Found out why when I got home.

The two dots appeared, like she was thinking of writing something else. He wandered over to his bed and sat down on the edge again, waiting. After what seemed like a long time to Brad, the phone buzzed again.

Want to go for coffee?

Brad blinked. *Yes.* Amy was as different from Candice as night and day. He really didn't want to make the same mistake twice; he had to somehow remain Amy's friend and keep his feelings to himself. All romantic thoughts aside, he really wanted to see her. *Sure. Second Cup on Livingstone?*

See you in 20?

I'll be there.

As Brad rushed around, changing his clothes, another thought occurred to him. He couldn't drive. He could take his car from the garage and hope that he didn't get caught, or he could do the right thing and either call Amy or take a bus or his bike. Swallowing, he opened his messages.

Can you come get me? My license is still suspended.

The reply was almost instant. Was she as excited to see him as he was her? They'd really been apart for only a few hours, but after the ranch, it felt like an eternity.

Sure, be there in ten.

CHAPTER TWENTY

True to her word, Amy appeared in an early model Toyota Corolla in only ten minutes. She took a deep breath before climbing from the car.

"Hey," she said. She felt shy away from the ranch.

"Hey," he said. Brad seemed unsure of himself, too. He slid his hands into the pockets of his freshly pressed jeans. The collar of his red polo shirt shifted over the skin of his neck revealing a sunburn.

"Ah, you ready?" she asked.

Before he walked back into the house to get his housekey, he stopped her with a hand to the arm. "Listen, thanks for doing this. I feel like such an idiot, but I don't want to get in trouble again."

Amy smiled. Maybe this friendship was going to be a bit harder than she'd anticipated. She shifted her hand through the strands of her straight, black hair.

"No worries. I needed some space from my parents."

"Parents? As in, plural?"

"Yeah, let's get in the car. I'll tell you on the way."

"Sure." Brad grabbed his phone, locked the front door, and slid the key into his pocket before ushering Amy to the car with a hand to her back.

Once they were seated and driving, Amy began. "My dad was home when I got there . . . "

Amy turned away from the shock in Brad's expression. She'd felt the same when she'd walked into the house with her mother and found her father awaiting them. The entire drive from Heavenly Haven, her mother hadn't uttered a word of warning. Amy didn't know whether it was the sight of her father or the smile on her mother's face as they entered that shocked her the most.

"He just stood there as if nothing had happened," she said. "Like he hadn't messed up our family at all with his actions. And my mother . . . " She hadn't known what to say to her mother. How could she? "I mean, what was she thinking? It's been only two weeks. Why isn't she angry with him?"

"Did you ask them?" Brad asked. His hand lifted from his thigh as if to reach out to her, but it stopped midair and returned to its place. An old jolt of longing swept through her, and she quickly pressed it down, but she wasn't quick enough. Warmth crept up her neck and to her face.

"No, I didn't say anything. I didn't know what to say. Just the sight of them together after everything that happened . . . " Her throat convulsed, and she desperately sought the tools Mildred had taught her to reach for when she was overwhelmed. Deep inhale, count to four, release, count to four. Repeat as needed. Eventually, her breaths came out easier. She glanced over at Brad and found him watching her. Then she had to start the exercise all over again.

Her heart continued to thunder through her veins. This time, it wasn't in panic. It had happened every time at the farm since Brad had agreed to be her "ex." It was a foreign feeling. Amy had never felt this way about anyone before. Yet somehow, in her time at Heavenly

Haven, she'd managed to do two things she never would have thought possible: find forgiveness and fall in love. And with a friend—someone she already knew! She wished he would take her hand like he'd done so many times, to show he was there, to show her she was safe. A thought occurred to her—would it also show that he cared about her, too?

Shaking her head at the crazy thought, she returned her attention to the road. They were two blocks away from the coffee shop, and although she'd lived in Bethel all her life, it seemed new and fresh—an unexplored adventure. Unable to contain the feeling, she grabbed Brad's hand, squeezing it quickly before letting go.

He sucked in a quick breath, face forward, gaze fixed on the road. Warm embarrassment flooded her, and she quickly stared forward again. Out of the corner of her eye she saw that Brad's expression was confused. What was he thinking?

Five minutes later, she brought the car to a stop outside The Second Cup coffee shop. She opened the door a little, surprised to see Brad already on the sidewalk waiting for her. Goodness, he was quick. Those long legs did him well. He offered her a hand, and she took it, having no expectation of hanging onto it once she was out of the car. But Brad didn't let go.

After he'd gestured for her to lock the car, he pulled her with him, keeping a comforting hold on her hand. It was nice and strange and totally impossible to remain unaffected. Her attraction to Brad could lead nowhere. He was her friend, and that was that. Forcing herself to ignore the feel of his palm against hers, she gently untangled their fingers.

Brad remained close to her side as they stood in line to place their orders, and then they sought an unused table at the back. Classical music swam over the din of voices. Small, round tables seated two or three people each. Some diners talked animatedly with their companions, and others stared, brows furrowed, into the depths of their computer screens, sipping drinks amidst furious typing. Deep green vinyl booths lined the back walls, and the smell of brewing coffee filled the air.

Upon hearing their names, Brad and Amy went to pick up their orders.

"So, Felicia's having a party tonight. Do you think we should go?" Brad asked a few minutes later as he sipped his cappuccino.

They'd chosen a window seat. The sun glared through the tinted windows, warming the vinyl. Second Cup was busy, true to its reputation. Amy's cup of chai tea hung between her cupped hands, and two fully loaded croissants rested on the table between them. She'd been surprised at Brad's choice of food. He had always struck her as burger type of guy. It seemed odd that he would pick a croissant instead.

"I think it might be nice to see everyone again and put whatever rumors are flying around to rest."

"Do you want to go together?" Brad asked, very interested in the small paper napkin underneath his croissant.

Amy choked a little on her tea. Was he serious? "I don't think . . . "

Brad shrugged, a red hue working up the side of his neck. "Just as friends," he stammered. "You know. Together in the same car. I don't really want to end up in a courtroom, and riding my bike in the dark might not be the best idea."

It made perfect sense. Friends. "Okay, sure. It will give me an excuse to get away from my parents, at least for the evening."

Brad nodded. "Great. Just come get me when you're ready."

"Okay, I'll send you a text when I'm on my way."

Amy sipped her tea, enjoying the mix of warmth and spice. The chamomile tea Mildred made at the farm was nice, but it was the only kind she had. It was nice to have something different, yet familiar. Her life had been anything but normal since that night at the party, and she now found a small sense of enjoyment in some of the things she'd previously taken for granted.

Brad was silent as they worked their way through the drinks and croissants, his expression faraway.

"Hey," she said. "Was your dad home?"

Brad's brow furrowed. "No, it seems my weekend visit was not reason enough to drag himself from whatever business is occupying his time."

He sighed and ran his hand through his dirty blond hair. "Ira, his driver, picked me up and brought me home. The house was empty when I got there."

Amy reached for his hand and took it in hers. "I'm sorry, Brad." He turned their hands over and gently weaved his fingers between hers. His grip was surprisingly tense.

"I suppose I shouldn't be surprised." He shrugged and then let out a heavy breath. "It just hurts, you know? Does he care at all?"

"I know we've only really gotten to know each other in the last two weeks—and I might be making a bad suggestion—but why don't you call your dad and speak to him? Maybe tell him how you feel?"

Brad's eyebrows rose so high, they were almost hidden by his hairline. "Now, why didn't I think of that?" he asked sarcastically. Amy pulled back. Regret immediately invaded his expression. "I'm sorry. It's just complicated. You're right. Maybe I should just call him."

Brad didn't look thrilled at the prospect. Amy understood how complicated parental relationships could be. "What about you and your parents? Are you going to tell them how you feel?"

She shrugged. "I don't know. I mean, I guess it isn't really my choice if my mother takes my father back or if he moved into the house again. I can see my actions did something to them, and maybe they really do need each other." She rubbed her eyes. "I don't know."

Brad chuckled and once more reached across the table for her fingers. "I guess we both have a lot to figure out." Was it just her, or was there a double meaning to his words? Brad suddenly cleared his throat and let go of her hand, taking up his coffee again.

"Do you think it will be awkward tonight?" he asked, placing his cup on the table again.

"Without a doubt," Amy answered.

CHAPTER TWENTY-ONE

B rad waved to Amy as she did a three-point turn in the drive and disappeared into the waning afternoon. He turned, noticing for the first time that the black BMW had been joined by another older car, which was silver with New York plates. It couldn't be his father's; he wouldn't be caught dead in a car like that.

He pushed open the front door, unsure what to expect, and came to an abrupt halt. Brad's father was wrapped in an intense embrace with a woman in a navy blue dress. Her long, red hair flowed over the arm wrapped around her back. Still dressed in his suit, Brad's father's jacket sleeves bunched around his muscles as he pulled the woman closer.

"Dad, what the are you doing?" Brad demanded.

The two sprang apart, as if someone had applied an electric shock. His father's cheeks matched the blushing woman's. She was almost as tall as his father, who was only a few centimeters shorter than Brad himself. Although he probably couldn't guess her age correctly, she was an older woman, though quite pretty. Her green eyes were fixed on Brad, and he saw that they were filled with wariness, shock, and something he could define only as compassion.

"Brad." His father cleared his throat, reaching for the woman and leading them closer to where Brad waited by the open door. "Why don't you close the door and join us in the sitting area?"

Brad couldn't move; his brain was screaming at him to do something, although his body was unable to respond.

"Brad," his father said again. "I'm going to ask Mrs. McCleary to make us some tea." He watched Brad, waiting for a response, his expression composed but his steely, gray eyes wary.

Brad nodded but didn't make a move toward the sitting area. Instead, he followed his father deeper into the house in search of Mrs. McCleary. His father stepped into the kitchen, talking in quiet tones to the housekeeper, and Brad suppressed the urge to verbalize the frenzy of emotions clawing at his chest.

How *could* he? Who was that woman, and what was she doing in their house? Brad wasn't so naïve as to think that his father had never touched, looked at, or dated another woman since his mother had passed. He'd never met any of his father's women, though, and none of them had ever set foot in the Thorn house—at least, to Brad's knowledge.

His father, done with whatever he'd been discussing with Mrs. McCleary, gestured for Brad to follow him from the kitchen and down the hallway back to the sitting room. Not a word passed between the two until the elder Thorn had taken his place beside the mysterious woman perched on the loveseat.

Brad paused at the door, swallowing hard. His father inclined his head toward the green, rounded chair opposite them, but Brad ignored him and leaned against the fireplace across the room instead. His father sighed softly, looking at the woman and taking her hand in his.

"Brad, as you know, your mother has been gone for—"

"What is this, Dad?" he interrupted. "Who is this woman?"

To Brad's immense surprise, his father didn't get angry—and he didn't yell, as he usually would have after such an outburst. Instead, he looked at the woman again, who swallowed nervously and gently nodded at him to continue.

"Brad, this is Danika," his father said, gazing at the woman the way he used to look at Brad's mother. Something twinkled in the weak sunlight streaming through the windows and caught Brad's roving gaze. Another jolt ran through his body. On Danika's left hand sparkled an emerald square cut diamond on a plain, gold band. "My wife."

Brad turned and ran for the door.

They gave him about twenty minutes, although hours might have easily passed as Brad lay on his bed, stewing over this new development. A quiet, precise knock sounded on his bedroom door before it swung open. Brad sprung to his feet, starting to pace in the distance from his bed to his gaming console.

"Now, Brad," his father said, entering, "that is not the way I expect you to behave, especially—"

Brad had heard enough. "Spare me, Dad. How did you think I would react to you bringing a strange woman home? Into our lives, into our house? Did you think about me before you two tied the knot? What about Mom? Don't you love her anymore?"

His father waited until Brad had spent all his words. He rubbed the skin between his eyes as his lips pressed into a thin line. "I will always love your mother, Brad. As for the rest, Danika is your stepmother, and I expect you to behave yourself. You are a Thorn, and you should act like it." Steel entered his father's voice.

Brad sagged back down onto his bed, sitting on the edge. A part of him hoped his father would sit beside him and talk to him like Griffin had done at Heavenly Haven. Brad knew that he wouldn't; that wasn't Adrian Thorn's style.

Instead, he shook his head, spun on his heel, opened the door, and stalked out, closing it firmly behind him. Brad guessed that the conversation was over. He unclenched his jaw and released a breath, flopping back onto his bed and staring at the ceiling until the shadows along the walls deepened. The clock in the hallway struck six. It was about time for the party. He couldn't wait for Amy to get there.

"Are you okay?" Amy asked as soon as Brad managed to fold himself into the passenger seat of her Corolla.

Was he? He didn't know. All he knew was that his jaw ached from clenching it, and his shoulders were so tight, it felt like he had spent five hours in the weight room and hadn't taken the time to stretch.

"Fine."

Amy nodded and turned onto the main road. The sun was setting over the town of Bethel, and a mirage of oranges and pinks spread across the sky. He belatedly noticed the sweet smell of Amy's perfume filling up the space in the car. He inhaled deeply, wishing he had the right to pull her over to him, wrap her in his arms, and spill all his secrets and burdens.

Once his anger had abated enough to think clearly, hurt sprang up in a fiery torrent in his chest. How could his father not have told him about Danika? He'd gotten married without even telling Brad that there was a woman he was serious about. Was this what their relationship had come to? Brad had hidden plenty from his father, and now it seemed his father had repaid the favor. His hands curled into tight fists until his knuckles shone white. Blood pumped through his veins, pounding a rhythm in his head.

It slowed as a soft hand slid over his, gently brushing over his skin until the tension in his hands relaxed. As his fingers uncurled, Amy entwined her fingers with his, quietly sharing his pain, offering support.

"My dad got remarried," he whispered hoarsely, "without even telling me."

"Oh, Brad, that must have been a shock! How did you find out?"

"You mean, after walking in on them making out?"

Amy made a sound of horror. "Ew. I'm sure that was gross!"

Despite his sour mood, Brad grinned. "Definitely not something I want burned into my memory." The levity went as quickly as it came. "I mean, how could he do this? He never even told me there *was* a woman, and then as soon as I'm out of the way, he decides to get married. Who does that?" Emotions pulsed through his veins once more, and the muscles in his jaw clenched so tightly, he was sure his teeth would crack under the pressure.

"The thing is," he continued, staring down at their joined hands, "I knew it would happen eventually. The part that bugs me the most is that he didn't tell me about her. He left me out of the wedding, probably because he knew I'd make a scene. It's like . . . he doesn't even want me in his life anymore." He sighed. "Like I'm nobody to him."

They pulled up to Felicia's house; and Amy brought the car to a stop, parked, and then turned to him, taking both his hands into hers. He could hear the steady rhythm of the drum beating in time with the music from the loudspeakers. A cacophony of voices rang into the night.

"You're not a nobody. You matter to me and to those people out there. You matter to us."

He gripped her hands tighter, wanting to pull her close, *needing* to hold her, needing to feel someone who cared about him holding him. He wanted to kiss her, but instead, he pulled her into his chest, wrapping her in his arms and buried his face in her hair. He inhaled her sweet scent of peaches and vanilla. Amy stiffened for a moment in surprise, then relaxed and held him tight. Something genuine and new washed over his anger and pain. He didn't want it to go, so he held on until he felt Amy loosen her arms from his middle and begin to pull back. He reluctantly let her go.

"Sorry," he muttered, trying without success to release his seat belt.

Amy cleared her throat. "Nothing to apologize for," she said, her voice slightly breathy. Maybe he'd held her too tightly.

Before he could apologize again, Amy pushed open her door and climbed from the car, revealing a tight pair of black jeans, a teal, patterned top that bared her shoulders, and her phone stuck in her back pocket. Shaking his head, he smiled. Too bad he couldn't tell her how great she looked. Instead, he climbed out of the car and prepared himself to face the party.

CHAPTER TWENTY-TWO

"Oh, my goodness! Amy! And Brad! It is so good to see you guys. We've been so worried," Felicia gushed as soon as they'd walked through the front door. Her soft pink, silk dress was splashed with color as the strobe light throbbed in time with the music.

Jace, his black t-shirt stretching across his impressive shoulders and his legs cased in dark blue jeans, waited beside her. One of his hands clutched Felicia's slim hip. For once, Amy didn't feel self-conscious standing next to Felicia. She was just glad to see her friend's smiling face again.

"Good to be seen," Amy said. Brad muttered something similar before taking the hand Jace offered and shaking it. Felicia and Jace watched the two of them appraisingly, and Amy decided to ignore the question clearly written on both of their faces.

"Are you ready to get your groove on?" Felicia asked Jace, swinging her hips, despite the firm hold he had on them. He seemed to really like Felicia, and Amy was happy for them. Jace grinned, gripped Felicia's hand, and dragged her back to the dance floor. Amy watched with amusement as the two disappeared into each other's gazes, lips meeting.

"Do you want something to drink?" Brad asked, his hand tight against the small of her back. She didn't think it was a territorial move or a statement, just nerves.

"Sure," she said. She appreciated the space Felicia and the others gave them. It was like any other day, any other party.

They walked toward the kitchen to get their drinks. As they entered the dimly lit room, Brad moved with familiarity. He held out a beer to her, snapping the cap of his own and taking a long swallow. As tied up as his emotions were, she wasn't surprised when a second bottle quickly followed the first. Brad, it seemed, was determined to drown his sorrows or pain—or whatever excuse he was telling himself.

"Don't you think you should leave off of that tonight?" she asked.

Brad gave her a sour look, shrugged, and reached for a bottle of water instead.

She tentatively took a sip of her drink. Before going to Heavenly Haven, she'd been a big drinker, taking anything she could get her hands on as often as she could. It was a coping mechanism, a place of peace. Now, as the alcohol slid down her throat in a battle of sweetness and fire, she didn't feel the need to guzzle it down as she once did. In fact, after this one, she would probably find some pop. Brad was working on his third drink. This one was a tall boy. He tipped the can to the other room, and she nodded. They should rejoin the party— after all, that was why they'd come—to see their friends.

She placed her almost-empty drink on a nearby table. Brad did the same and wrapped his arm around her waist, the dark green cotton material of his button-up bunching at her back. "Do you want to dance?"

"Sure." She allowed him to pull her close, listening to the steady thump of his heart against her ear as they moved to the melody of the music. It felt nice to be held by Brad. It wasn't the same as dancing with a boy that had no interest in her other than her body. It was better, being with someone who knew some of her deepest secrets, shared her pain, and wanted to be her friend, anyway.

She looked up, meeting Brad's dark blue eyes, feeling mesmerized. His long legs brushed hers as she rested against the hands at her back. Music wove between them, everything else fading into the background. He leaned closer until only inches remained between them. The air stripped itself from her lungs. Was he going to kiss her? Here? Now? In front of all of their friends? Did she mean something to him, just like he was rapidly becoming someone important to her?

Her eyes slid closed, and she thought she heard a happy sound escape Brad. His breath brushed her lips. "Amy . . . "

The song switched to another. As the opening bars belted into the room, Amy felt a shiver run down her spine—and not from the pleasure of being so close to Brad. A shiver that was made of anything but delight. Her palms began to sweat. She had to get out of here; she was in danger. The bass drum rolled, pounding her blood in her limbs. Calm fled, panic taking its place. She gasped desperately. Pushing Brad's arms away, she fled the room. He didn't let her get far.

"Amy! Amy, I'm sorry," Brad said, reaching for her, resting a hand loosely on her hip. "Amy, look at me."

A stutter of static crashed over the music, silencing the melody. Memories assaulted her in the silence. The music that night. The bottle. The glass. Her blood, so much blood. And then darkness.

Tremors of fear spread like spasming muscles through her back and chest, rushing blood through her limbs. Dizziness blurred her vision, and nausea swirled in her stomach. She felt the alcohol she'd just consumed creeping its way up her throat. She swallowed hard, forcing it back down. "I have . . . I have to . . . "

"Amy." Brad gripped her arms, driving her through the kitchen and out the back door, into the darkness outside. They followed the stone path in Felicia's garden to a quiet spot when the music came back to life, suddenly soft in the background. Fresh, cool air slapped her cheeks, and reason returned to her mind.

"Amy?" The worry in Brad's voice reached through the fog.

Sweet oxygen flowed into her lungs. She gasped, sucking it in and counting to three. "What happened?" she asked. Her knees barely had the strength to support her, and she rested her spinning head against Brad's chest. His warmth soaked into her freezing limbs as he wrapped her in a tight hug.

"I don't know; you suddenly freaked out. What was it?" Brad asked, moving them both to sit on the grass-covered ground. He sat and pulled her between his legs, cradling her close to him until her shoulder touched his chest. She allowed it, grateful for his steadiness, and tried to center her thoughts.

"Give me a minute."

Brad nodded, lapsing into silence, his arms firmly around her. Gently, he ran his hand down her hair and back, a tingling trail of sparks following his hand. Amy closed her eyes and tried to remember. The song. It was the same one that had played the night she'd scarred her wrists.

"I think it was the song—I remember it because the same one was playing when I . . . when I . . . " She pointed to her wrists. "It was . . . triggering. Mildred had explained something like that to me." She'd said that a sensory experience could evoke a bad memory, but this was scarier and more sudden than Amy had imagined. "It brought back all those feelings from that night."

Brad's eyes widened in understanding. "Oh, man, Amy, no wonder you freaked out." He shuddered, pressing his face firmly against her hair. His arms were a tight band of protection around her. "I can't imagine how scary that must've been."

"Yeah, I didn't make a conscious connection. I just kind of followed through with the feeling. I was so lonely then, and the pain . . . It was . . . "

Brad's steady gaze met hers, and he nodded, sympathy filling his soft blue eyes. "I understand that all too well." He did. Brad was familiar with the feelings that would drive someone to an act like that. "You know you aren't alone anymore. I'm here for you." He lifted his hand to her chin, lifting her face so that his gaze met hers. "Anytime."

"Me, too," she said softly.

The air around them grew thick with tension. Rational thought drained faster the longer his gaze remained focused on her. She should move away. Relationships at Heavenly Haven were against the rules, and when the weekend was over, they would be returning for two more weeks. Nothing could happen between them; it would be disastrous.

Despite all the reasons she gave herself in defense of why this couldn't happen, she didn't pull out of Brad's embrace, didn't stop him as he bent his head closer to hers. When his mouth met hers, she kissed him back.

He knew kissing her would be a bad idea. The sudden fear that had overtaken the sensible part of Brad's brain, dampened by the alcohol swimming in his blood, was heightened at the thought of a world where Amy did not exist.

Pushing aside the terrible timing of this revelation, he deepened the kiss and ignored all of his conflicting thoughts. His timing was bad—really bad. They both still had so much baggage to deal with, but as her lips moved against his, even those reasons were wiped from his mind. Minutes passed. With great reluctance, he broke the kiss before things got out of hand.

Amy pressed her face into his shoulder as they quietly regained their breath. The silence was filled with all that had been said and all that needed to be said. Neither broke it. Perhaps it was the hope that they could have this, that they might be together—and somehow pave the way for something beautiful when both of them were ready—when the baggage they both carried was dealt with.

But life was rarely perfect. He would worry about tomorrow when he had to. He held Amy for a long time, his heart slowing into a steady rhythm. Then, by mutual consent, they rejoined the others at the party, careful to keep their distance and act like nothing momentous had occurred between them. After all, they were just friends.

CHAPTER TWENTY-THREE

"Drums Keep Pounding a Rhythm Through My Brain" by Nancy Sinatra circled in Brad's own brain as he forced his eyelids open with a loud groan. Bright sunlight streamed through his uncovered windows, and judging by the sun's position, it was almost noon. His head ached, and the familiar sourness of too much alcohol lingered in his mouth.

He sat up, gritting his teeth as waves of dizziness pressed against his vision. Where was he? A quick scan of his surroundings told him he was in his bed, but the funny thing was that he didn't remember coming home. The last memory he had was of Amy—dancing with her and fighting the urge to kiss her again. It had been hard to resist, and Amy seemed to feel the same; but each time he thought of trying again, she would step away from him in warning. If he pushed it, she would run away, and then who knew what would happen to him?

In two quick swallows, he emptied the bottle of water at his bedside and then gulped back the nausea that lurched in his gut. In a flurry of color, recollections surged into focus. He'd come home from the party, happy and content, and then he'd run into his dad and Danika again. They were in the kitchen. Unsurprisingly, with the amount of booze swimming in his blood, there had been no filter or common sense to hold him back. Like a fire, anger ignited inside him, and decency and restraint left. Words spilled from his lips in a torrent of pain and fury, and wrath from his father followed.

Although he couldn't precisely remember what vitriol had passed between them, he remembered the cool weight of his keys between his fingers, Danika pleading for him to stop, the roar of the truck's engine, and the burning drink flowing down his throat. Sickness crawled up from his stomach, his gut tightening until there was nothing for it but to run for the bathroom to relieve himself of the poison.

Disgust at his actions the night before leaked like tiny tears along with the sweat on his brow. He wiped them away. Griffin's face brushed his thoughts. He cringed. The thought of returning to Heavenly Haven later that day and sharing the news of his failure sat like lead in the pit of his empty stomach. But who could blame him? His life was a mess. There was no one to hold him accountable; and judging from his relationship with his father, this would be the life he would inevitably live. So, why bother trying to change it?

He pushed himself to standing and moved to the basin, splashing cold water on his face before thinking better of it and heading for the shower. Ten minutes later, he was dressed, small droplets of water dripping down into the collar of his shirt from his hair. He grabbed his car keys and headed out the door.

"Amy."

Amy went rigid at the sound of her father's voice breaking into her thoughts of Brad and the night before. She sat at the edge of her bed with her phone resting in her palm. Her room felt different to her somehow—like a space that she knew but didn't quite belong to anymore.

"Dad?" she asked, turning around. It wasn't like she'd purposefully gone out of her way to avoid her dad; it was more that they kept occupying different spaces.

"Can we talk?"

Reluctantly, Amy nodded to the edge of her bed, and her father took a seat.

Eventually, her father sighed. "What happened between your mother and me is unusual. I know it must have been difficult for you to come home expecting one thing and finding another." He let out another deep breath. "But you scared us, Amy. I've never been so terrified in my life as when we got the call from Jace . . . " He broke off, tears choking his voice.

"I'm sorry, kiddo," he whispered, hesitantly drawing her into his side. She allowed her father to surround her in a hug. "I know it will take some time for you to forgive me—or maybe you never will—but please remember that I love you and Logan. I love your mother. No matter what happens between us in the future, please know that we are here for you and Logan, whatever you need. You are never alone."

It was hard to hear her father's words with the weight of the anger between them still lingering in the air like a bad smell. He still didn't know the full reason that she'd thought taking her life was easier than living it.

"Dad, I need to tell you something . . . "

"Whatever it is, Amy, I will still love you."

She wanted so badly to believe those words, to believe that her father's love and acceptance would still be there when she unveiled her secret. Only time would tell, and later, she would be on her way back to Heavenly Haven.

So, she told him.

CHAPTER TWENTY-FOUR

He should be asleep. All around Brad, the campers at Heavenly Haven lay oblivious to him in their tents. Tonight, they were on some bonding activity, something Griffin had thought out. His discussion with Griffin about the weekend happenings was uncomfortable, but aside from reinforcing the rules of Heavenly Haven about the use of alcohol, Griffin was supportive, reaffirming his belief in Brad.

Apparently, being in the middle of nowhere in a tent with a blazing fire was good for the soul. Well, the fire was nice—the hard ground, not so much. Brad stared longingly at the tent he knew Amy shared with Bethany. She was no doubt asleep. She'd seemed troubled earlier. He wished she would tell him why—maybe she still would.

After the events of the weekend, though, their relationship had changed. Amy seemed unsure of him. The weekend certainly had changed a lot for him. Did Amy feel the same, or was he alone in this? Staying away from her was turning out to be harder than he had imagined.

When he'd seen her laughing at something Mildred had said as they assembled outside the main farmhouse, piling the necessities into heavy backpacks for their campout that night, it had taken all he possessed not to run to her side and throw his arms around her. He'd had to force his attention to his pack, studiously loading a change of clothes, a sleeping bag, food, and other odds-and-ends they needed, rather than giving into the impulse.

He sighed. Maybe a walk would tire him out. Doubtful, since an eight-kilometer hike hadn't. He grabbed a flashlight, quietly unzipped his tent, and climbed out, rezipping it. The moonlight showed the trail as clear as day. It wasn't difficult to see. It was well-walked. Just how many sets of feet at Heavenly Haven had walked along the same ground?

The night was cool and the sky black, shot up like a pin board with spots of white and yellow. Winter was slowly giving way to spring. The crickets were chirping their happy songs. An owl hooted in the night somewhere, and he paused, shining his flashlight into the darkened trees. It wasn't that the dark scared him. It didn't—although, it was unnerving to walk alone between the shadows of spruce trees that surrounded him like a percussion of giants peering down on him from unspeakable heights.

The camp was out of sight when he heard a gravelly voice to his left. "Hey, kid," the voice said. "What're you doing out here alone?"

Brad turned and raised the flashlight higher. Light pooled between the trees, giving a face to the rough-looking man walking toward him. The bottom half of his face was covered with a dark brown beard, his expression open and friendly. His clothes were typical of a hiker, Brad thought: a red flannel overshirt, jeans, and hiking boots.

"You camping?" Brad said.

The man nodded and lifted a half-full bottle to his lips. Brown liquid—a brand with which Brad was familiar—glowed in the flashlight beams. Brad's eyes moved along the bottle. His mouth watered for a sip of it.

"Ah, where's your camp?"

The man drank from the bottle again and wiped his mouth with the sleeve of his shirt. "A mile down the path that way." The man gestured with a waving hand. Not far, then. Did he dare? No one would know. *Don't do it, Brad.*

He ignored the warning. "Mind if I join you?" he asked, gesturing to the bottle in the man's hand.

"Aren't you a little young?"

He laughed. "I'm old enough." He certainly didn't *feel* young.

"In that case, m' name's Hank." The man wobbled, his shoulder brushing close against a wide trunk as he climbed over a small bush.

"Brad," he said before following. The bottle called to him. He needed the burning liquid more than he needed sleep. Maybe after a few sips, sleep would find him that much easier. Besides, no one would know. Sunrise was hours away, and he would be back at camp in his tent long before that.

Hank bustled with surprising ease through the dark undergrowth. Despite his inebriated state, he obviously knew where he was going. Soon, they came to a campsite. A happy fire burned in the pit, and beside it, another man sat. He, too, held a bottle. This man had wide shoulders, blond hair, and blue eyes. Brad wondered for a moment if the blond man had ever been a linebacker—he certainly had the build for it. The thought held him for only a moment before his gaze was drawn back to the bottle.

"You want one?" Hank asked, pointing to the bottle in the blond man's hands.

Brad sucked in a breath. He shouldn't. He should turn around, go back to his camp, and go to sleep. Then the smell of alcohol hit his nose.

"Sure," he said hoarsely, clearing his guilt from his throat.

Hank grinned and tapped the chair beside him. "Take a seat; the party's just beginning."

The glass was cold against his skin, the liquid cool as it filled his mouth. Indeed, the party had just begun.

"Brad." Someone shook his shoulder. "Brad, wake up! What are you doing here?" The shaking continued, and he groaned.

Who was shaking him, and why wouldn't they leave him alone? "Go away," he murmured.

"Brad Thorn, you get up right now or else. I am sorely tempted to find a bottle of water and use it."

Brad's brain kicked in, and his eyes blinked open. The sun was bright, piercing what felt like nails into his head as his eyes adjusted to the blur of light and color above them. A curtain of blue-black hair shadowed his eyes from the sun, and sapphire blue eyes looked down at him with a mixture of concern and fury. "Amy, why are you in my tent?"

Amy's gaze narrowed, the fire in them all but spitting. "I am not in your tent. I came to wash up and found you passed out on the ground."

"On the ground in my tent?" he asked.

Amy bent closer, sniffed, and moved back again with a frown. "You've been drinking. And no, we are *not* in your tent."

"Will you help me get there? I think I need some sleep."

Amy slid her arm under his armpits and struggled with him to her feet. "I'm going to take you to your tent and leave you there. You can explain to Griffin if he meets us on the way."

"And then I can sleep," Brad said.

Amy sighed loudly in his ear, gripping him tightly around the waist. They wobbled. Brad's feet were not working properly, and his head felt like it was stuffed with cotton. Thankfully, when they reached the camp, it was quiet, the other campers still sleeping restfully. All but he and Amy. The zipper of his tent flap whizzed loudly in the quiet morning, and he dropped to his knees and crawled inside. Without another word, Amy zipped it closed behind him. He put his head on his pillow and was instantly asleep.

They were in the middle of nowhere. How had Brad found alcohol? Amy stared at the blue and lime green domed tent before her, worry punching her gut. She shook her head and pushed to her feet, walking quickly back down the path to where she had found Brad. She retrieved her towel and water bottle and inhaled deeply. The air was so clean and fresh in the mountains. A bird twittered in a tall tree. She turned to watch it launch itself into the bleeding sky from its perch on the branch of a giant pine tree. She watched it cross the sky, trailing it with her eyes until it passed over the horizon, and then she was face to face with Griffin.

"Amy, I was just looking for you."

"Oh, why?"

"I went to check on Brad last night, but his bed was empty. I, uh . . . " Griffin's face heated. "You wouldn't happen to know anything about that, would you?"

Amy gasped, heat flooding her cheeks. She should tell Griffin where she'd found Brad. It would be the right thing to do. But what would happen to Brad? He was already on a warning. The truth or the lie? Amy gave into an old habit that had kept her safe over the years and lied. "Ah, yeah, we did go for a walk—nothing else. Just a walk. To talk." She drew a deep breath. "We're just friends, Griffin." And the lies kept coming.

"Oh," Griffin said, nodding slowly. He waved and turned back to the camp. "Thanks for letting me know."

Amy hurried to catch up with his long stride. She had sincerely hoped that Griffin would leave Brad for a few hours—at least long enough to sleep off whatever he'd had to drink the night before. But to her dismay, Griffin walked straight up to Brad's tent, opened the zipper, and peeked inside. Brad was out cold, his handsome face relaxed in sleep. She didn't know how much of his sleep could be attributed to exhaustion and how much to the alcohol in his body.

"Brad," Griffin said, shaking Brad's foot. "Rise and shine. It's time to pack up camp and move on." Brad didn't stir. Griffin climbed into the tent and shook Brad's shoulder this time.

"Brad, it's time to get up."

Brad groaned loudly. "What? I just got to sleep."

It was clear the moment Griffin smelled the alcohol on Brad's breath because he turned to Amy. His brow bent into a deep "V," and his mouth pressed into a hard line.

They were in so much trouble.

CHAPTER TWENTY-FIVE

B rad stared hard at Amy. This was his second trip to Griffin's office, and he sincerely doubted that it would end like his first. Mildred had come to camp to fetch them while Griffin and John led the rest of the campers on to the next night's camping site. Amy hadn't said two words to him, and in his anger, he had kept it that way.

After arriving, Mildred marched them into Griffin's office to "talk" about what had happened. Mildred sat in Griffin's chair, her usually friendly face set in an unhappy line.

"I guess I don't need to tell you just how much lying"—she nodded to Amy—"and substance abuse are frowned upon at Heavenly Haven." She nodded to Brad. Brad felt his stomach sink to his shoes. Now that he was lucid enough to remember what had happened the night before, the alcohol sat like a sour weight in his stomach. He mimicked Amy's pose and studied his hiking boots. Amy didn't lift her head.

"Brad, I would like you to wait outside the office while I deal with Amy."

A small hitch caught Amy's breath, and her shoulders rounded, as if she was trying to fold in on herself. He wanted to comfort her, but he held himself back. He was sure Amy had sold him out to Griffin. Otherwise, how else would Griffin have known? He'd asked Amy, but she'd refused to answer. She was angry with him—of that he had no doubt—but angry enough to tell Griffin?

"Fine." He wished Amy would look him in the eye. At least then, he would have some idea of what was going on in her head. He tried one last time to catch her eye, but she stayed where she was, head bowed down over her hands. He slid his hands into the front pockets of his jeans as he stood and left the room.

Flopping down into a pale blue chair outside the office, he leaned his head against the headrest and closed his eyes. It seemed like only moments had passed when Amy hurried back out of the office, sniffling.

"Amy," he said, reaching out to stop her. His hand brushed her arm, but she ripped it away. If he needed any more proof of her guilt, he had it. Why else would she not look him in the eye? Why else wouldn't she answer his questions?

"Brad, please come in," Mildred said. As always, her voice was kind, but he could hear a hint of sternness underneath the kindness. There was no doubt in his mind that he would be going home today. It was time to pay the piper. He wandered back into the office and slouched into the seat he'd sat in earlier. It wasn't particularly comfortable. The back was too short, hitting him in the middle. The sides were round, almost like a saucer, and the strange purple color was not his favorite. The cushion still felt soft, but it was flat, like many people had sat in it. He gazed out the window until Mildred cleared her throat, drawing his attention.

"Brad, at Heavenly Haven, we try to provide a growing environment for those who come here. That said, we have strict rules to ensure that the environment we maintain is kept in such a manner. The first night you were here, you drank yourself into oblivion, and we decided to give you a second chance because it was clear you needed it. After your altercation with Alex, you were warned that if you broke any more of the rules, you would be sent home.

"I have been informed that last night, you were drunk while on the campout; and despite Griffin's pleas for mercy, I have no choice but to send you home. I have notified your father, and he will be along to fetch you in a few hours."

"Please, I need to—" Brad lurched forward in his chair.

Mildred held up a firm hand, her expression severe, but compassion brimmed her wizened eyes. "I'm sorry, Brad. You have left me no choice in this matter." Her face softened. "I hope someday, you will be able to take what you have learned in these weeks and find peace. I will pray for you."

Brad nodded. There was no point in arguing. He stood and walked slowly from the office, down the long, dusty road back to the cottage. He would miss Heavenly Haven. He deeply regretted not staying in his tent last night and trying to sleep. He never should have gone to the man's camp and taken that bottle, but it was too late to take it back now.

The cottage door opened with its usual squeak, and he crossed the carpet to his room. In a daze, he packed up his clothes. Brad reached for the Bible Griffin had given him that first night. Should he take it? Something told him he would need it, and this time, he heeded that voice. With the room empty, he zipped up his bag and placed it on the floor beside him. All he could do now was wait.

A few minutes later, the cottage door opened with another squeak. Brad jumped to his feet. His father had gotten here a lot quicker than he'd thought . . .

His feet stuttered to a halt when someone else entirely awaited him. "What are you doing here?" he demanded.

Amy's already white skin paled further, and she swallowed hard. "I came to see how you were."

"You mean, you came so that you can feel better about selling me out to Griffin?"

Amy's blue eyes widened in disbelief and anger. "What?"

"Tell me, Amy, did it make you feel like a hero, telling Griffin your poor, pathetic friend couldn't hold his liquor? To prove to him what a screwup I am?" Anger heated his blood. "Well, let me tell you, I don't need any of you. So what if I drink a little bit or get drunk? I'm going through a lot. I thought you, of everyone, would understand that. I need something to help me to relax. And who are you to preach, Amy? I thought you cared about me. What happened to the other night?" Emotion choked his voice.

Tears spilled down Amy's cheeks, and she shook her head vigorously, denying his words. "I didn't say anything to Griffin."

"You're lying." Molten heat flowed into him and combusted. He grabbed Amy's arm, pulling her face close to his. She'd hurt him; he could feel something inside him tearing apart. As he gazed into her eyes, he saw her fear. She was afraid of him. Like being splashed with icy water, his fury melted into guilt. He gently let go and stepped back. His hand busily moved through his hair. "I'm sorry," he muttered.

In a broken whisper, her voice reached out him. "Brad, I care about you, and I hope that you still consider me a friend. You and I both know you have a problem. Until you are willing to give up your crutch, you will never start healing from that pain you carry."

Her words struck him like a bolt of lightning. He didn't want to see her or the pleading in her eyes. "Please leave." He turned his back on Amy, went into the bedroom, and shut the door. He leaned against it, heart pounding and knees weak from fatigue. For a long moment, there was silence, and then, with a squeak, the front door opened and closed. Amy was gone.

Brad covered his eyes with his hands and gulped down deep breaths against the pain ripping like a vortex through his chest. Man, he wished he had a drink to make the pain go away, to numb it. It was easier than feeling.

The sunlight continued to move across the window. The door opened a second time, about half an hour after Amy left. Brad wearily stood to his feet, lifting his bag to his shoulder. As he opened his bedroom door, he wasn't at all surprised to see Ira, his father's driver, waiting for him in the living room. After all, why would his father take the time to fetch his messed-up son? He never had before.

Without a word, Brad followed Ira into the afternoon light. His gaze swept the farm, and he felt a pang of regret. He would miss this place. He would miss Griffin and his jokes, his tireless encouragement, and his belief that Brad could be more. If the people here at Heavenly Haven couldn't help someone like him, then no one could. Griffin was the one who had reported him, with Amy's help—but maybe he only said those things because he had to.

The pang inside him turned to pain. And Amy. She'd said she cared about him, but did she really? Obviously not enough to warn him.

He closed the cottage door and slipped into the backseat of the black BMW. Ira started the engine as Brad closed his eyes. He kept them closed all the way home.

CHAPTER TWENTY-SIX

Brad's outburst had hurt, although Amy understood that his anger wasn't really aimed at her. He was mad at himself, at his mistakes; she could see the desperation in his eyes. Amy sighed and twisted her hands together in her lap, wishing she knew a way to help Brad. Her words had hurt him; but she knew that for as long as he punished himself for his mistakes, the past would win again and again.

She'd experienced the same thing until she'd taken the past by the hand and presented it to her parents. They were furious about what Logan's friend had done to her, and after they had all cried about it, the two of them had promised to deal with it while she was away. There was no condemnation—only compassion and understanding. It felt good to get the secret out and help her parents to understand why she had been in such a dark place, why she'd made the choices she had . . . and everything in between. It was all working itself out, and Amy knew that she and her parents could face any further challenges together. It was a step toward healing for all of them.

Mildred was busy in the kitchen as usual as Amy entered the farmhouse. Across the counter lay a multitude of ingredients for cookies. "Penny for your thoughts."

"I just went to say goodbye to Brad. He . . . " She swallowed back her sorrow, squeezing her eyes tightly closed so that the tears wouldn't run down her cheeks.

"Sometimes, this calling comes with hard decisions. I will pray for Brad."

She hurt for him. The time they'd spent at Heavenly Haven had started the process of healing for both of them—though she knew Brad's journey was far from complete, much like her own.

"Could we do that? Pray, I mean?" she said.

"Of course—we can do that right now. Would you like to pray?"

Would she? For Brad, she would. Even if she wasn't sure if God would hear her. She bowed her head and spoke the simple words in her heart.

God, please help Brad. He needs You. Amen.

As she opened her eyes, Mildred lifted her head, her eyes compassionate. "Be at peace, Amy; there is no better place to leave those we care about than in the hands of our Savior," she said. Mildred took Amy's hand, smoothing her fingers gently over Amy's. Could Jesus really help Brad? And what about her? Was Jesus the answer to her peace?

"Yes, I suppose you're right," she said and carefully extracted her hands from Mildred, turning toward the recipe book. Of all the strange emotions she could identify spiraling through her at that moment, the words she'd heard so often in Mrs. Vaughn's class were slowly moving from her head to her heart: "'I have loved you with an everlasting love; I have drawn you with unfailing kindness'" (Jer. 31:3) and "I will never leave you nor forsake you" (Josh. 1:5b).

"It's just you and me for the next two days. How about you and I and make some cookies?" Mildred smiled. What would it be like to have the assurance and peace that Mildred exuded daily? Maybe it would help her to be honest with Mildred about Brad, her father, and everything else that seemed to be hanging over her this evening.

Together, they walked to the kitchen, and silently, Mildred went from cupboard to cupboard, handing off ingredients to Amy as she circled the room. Amy cleared her throat and began to talk.

"It won't help, you know," Danika said quietly. She took a seat opposite Brad at Harry's, settling her long black skirt carefully around her knees.

Two days had passed since his return from Heavenly Haven. It was not the first time she'd sought him out. On his return, his father hadn't said much, which surprised Brad almost as much as Danika's desire to talk to him. He'd shoved her off two more times, told her to mind her own business; and yet, here she was—sitting next to him at a bar, while the pitter patter of rain banged against blacked-out windows.

"What?" he asked flippantly.

"The drink won't help the pain—believe me."

Brad stared at her. Her red hair was styled in its usual elegance, and she was dressed to perfection, probably on his father's dime. But her eyes—they were so different from his father's. They held a compassion that reminded him of Heavenly Haven.

"Yeah, I don't know—it seems pretty good to me."

Danika sighed, but the soft light in her eyes didn't leave. "If I asked you to accompany me somewhere, would you go?"

"Ask my dad to go. I'm sure he'd love to go with you." Sarcasm dripped from his words. "Why are you here, anyway? I'm sure my dad didn't send you to find me. He would be last person to come and see if I'm all right."

"That's where you're wrong, Brad. Both you and your father suffer from the same malady—but that is not a discussion to be had tonight. Will you come with me?"

"So, you're a doctor now?" His words were callous. He wanted to take them back but couldn't bring himself to apologize. What did she want?

"Actually, I am, but that doesn't matter now. Your father is suffering from grief, just like you are. His way of dealing with it is working and maintaining control. Your way, it seems, is drinking and making bad decisions."

"And that makes it all better, does it?"

Danika reached out across the table and touched his clenched fist lightly with her finger. "No." She nodded to herself and then withdrew her hand. "Your father is working, and I would like you to come with me, please."

Amy's pleading face suddenly flashed through his mind, her voice begging—demanding—for him to be more than he was, better than he was.

"Okay," he said heavily. He slapped a bill on the table and then followed Danika from the bar, unsure of what he had agreed to do.

"Where are we going?" he asked. Danika gestured to her car, and he nodded. He was over the limit and still driving without a license. Without a word of complaint, he climbed into the passenger seat and shut the door behind him. Then they were on their way.

Danika tapped her hand on the steering wheel in time with the music. "If it's all right with you, I will tell you when we get there."

It made no sense to him, but he leaned back into his seat and let his mind wander back to Amy. What was she doing? Was Alex leaving her alone? Did she think of him as much as he thought of her? He rubbed his hand down his face.

In the few weeks he'd been at Heavenly Haven, the tight knot of guilt that had driven him for so long had slowly begun to lessen. Talking to Griffin about Candice had helped him to see that there was only one way that he could be free of it completely. He had made the decision to go and see her, talk to her, and beg her to forgive him for hurting her. Maybe if he could fix things with Candice, he would be one step closer to being someone who could be worthy of Amy.

Thirty minutes later, Danika brought the car to a stop outside a place called Save a Life Crisis Center. His eyes widened at the emblem of a mother and baby cuddled together beside the name. "Are you pregnant?"

Danika chuckled softly. "No, that's not the reason we're here. On Tuesday and Thursday nights, the center has an Alcoholics Anonymous meeting. There was a man here a few years ago whose story is very similar to yours. He is speaking to the group tonight, and I thought you might like to hear to what he has to say."

He wanted to say no; but Amy appeared in his thoughts again, and he nodded. "Okay."

He must have surprised Danika because she watched him for a moment before sliding the gear shift into park and climbing from the car. Brad did the same, curling his hands into his pockets as he walked. So many different emotions plagued him. It was as if he had held all his emotions in a vault and the thick walls were slowly beginning to crack. Emotions slid, one by one, through the holes. It was painful, like a wound that had been ripped open after scabbing over.

The building was almost silent as they entered. The hallways were dark except for one light to the left of the reception area. Danika seemed to know her way around, and he would ask her why later. Right now, as he followed her to a brightly lit room, he was too focused on his own uneasy feelings, anxiety roiling in his gut.

As he entered, surprise stopped him in his tracks. Danika continued, unaware of Brad's turmoil, over to where Griffin stood speaking to a group of men around Brad's age. The two embraced; they must be friends. Danika turned with Griffin and gestured to Brad. Griffin nodded and smiled. A good sign, he hoped. A moment later, the two were crossing the room to where he waited.

"It's good to see you, Brad," Griffin said, shaking his hand with a firm grip.

"And you," Brad said, shaking his head. "What are you doing here?"

"Remember when I told you my story?"

Brad nodded. It was frightening how much Griffin's story sounded like his own, yet Griffin hadn't ended up like Brad. He hadn't let the alcohol consume him. He had fought back—and with God's help, he had won.

"This is the group I attended to help me come clean after a stint in rehab. I am glad you came tonight. Since you left the farm, I have been praying for you, and my prayers have been answered with some help from Dr. Danika Peterson."

"It's Thorn now," Danika said, "I am a psychologist." Brad nodded. He would process this new revelation a bit later.

"I don't know about *answered*. I came under a misconception that Danika needed my help."

"Well," Danika said, "in a way, I do, but at a later date. When you are sober."

Really? What could Danika possibly need from him? A burly, bald man with tattoos on both his arms clapped his pan-sized hands together, drawing everyone's attention.

"If everyone can please take a seat, we will begin this evening's meeting."

People shuffled around and sat in rows of black metal seats near the closest wall. Brad took a seat beside Danika.

"My name is Ed, and tonight, we have a special guest who has come to speak to us about his own journey to sobriety. Please help me welcome Griffin Matthews."

Brad applauded along with the rest of the group. He'd heard Griffin's story before, but the second hearing was no less powerful than the first. Brad listened with rapt attention as something inside him yearned for what Griffin had.

CHAPTER TWENTY-SEVEN

Another wave crashed against the shores of Westwood. Brad stood, arms akimbo and eyes closed, and breathed in the salty air. The wind whispered through his sky blue t-shirt and khaki shorts and swirled the white sand around his bare feet. Westwood was beautiful, and he could feel the peace seeping like water into his dry soul.

A loud sigh escaped him as he looked over the crashing teal waters. He wished Amy were here to enjoy the sight with him, but like Candice, he had tossed her aside when the going got tough, too scared of himself to take the chance and make something better for himself—something better than his father and all his money could provide, at least.

That was the reason he had come here—to make peace with the past so he could make something better of his future. He sincerely hoped that this future included a dark-haired beauty who had somehow become important to him during the worst season of his life.

He clawed his hair back onto his head, sweeping the mass away from his eyes before letting it settle into an untidy mess. A few weeks ago, he would have been obsessed with keeping it styled and in place, but he no longer cared for such things. If there was one thing he had learned in his short time at Heavenly Haven, it was that worldly stuff was only temporary, but what he couldn't see was eternal. Griffin had taught him that.

He clenched his jaw, remembering the sadness and understanding he had seen in the older man's eyes when he had told Brad that he had to leave. It had hurt Griffin just like it had hurt Brad. Brad only wished he would have seen the destruction he had caused sooner. It was too late for him to return to Heavenly Haven, but due to Griffin's faith in him—daily emails of encouragement which had started the night after he'd gone with Danika and begun attending AA meetings—it was not too late for him to be sober. He was working at it.

First, he had to give up the bottle and then make peace with the reason he began drinking. He slid his phone from his pocket and glanced down at the time, turning to see the familiar features of Candice walking down the pathway toward him, Jack Anson at her side. She smiled at him. Instead of the insane jealousy he'd felt the first time he'd seen the two together, he realized he was happy for her, happy that Jack had taken his promise seriously and was living it out with Candice.

A few feet away from him, the two came to a stop. Brad drew a deep breath as he took in Candice's very pregnant figure. Jack didn't smile; he watched Brad impassively, protectively taking his stance at Candice's side.

"Brad," he said, his long arms crossed over his chest. It was an obvious warning.

Irrational heat beat through his body. He let it swirl and then let it go. He had no right to be angry with Jack. The last time he and Candice had spoken, only hateful words had passed between them. Brad winced at the memory of that last day Candice had walked the halls of Bethel, feeling the heat of shame flow into his neck and face.

"Hi, Jack." He turned and smiled tentatively at an anxious Candice, who was holding Jack's tense bicep. "Hi, Candice."

"Hi, Brad." She swallowed. "I have to admit, I was really surprised when Mrs. Potter phoned me to tell me you were looking for me and wanted to talk."

He was, too; it had taken a lot of promises—and downright begging—to get Mrs. Potter to agree to give him Candice's number. In the end, she must have heard he was sincere in wanting to make peace with Candice.

He rubbed the back of his neck, suddenly unsure. "I came to say I'm sorry," he began, "about . . . " A loud breath escaped him. "About everything. I'm sorry for hurting you, sorry for asking you to get rid of the baby, and sorry that I wasn't a better boyfriend."

Silence settled between them. Candice and Jack exchanged a long, meaningful look. Jack nodded slightly, a smile softening his lips as Candice smiled. The two were obviously very much in love, and he was grateful again for Jack Anson.

"Oh, Brad," Candice said, releasing her hold on Jack and walking over to him, her steps slow and careful. "I already forgave you a long time ago. But if you need to hear the words . . . " She took his hands in hers and waited until he met her eyes. "I forgive you, Brad."

Deep relief, like rain, swept away the muddy pain and guilt that he had carried for so long. The showers disappeared, and rays of sunshine shone over his soul, warming the place of sorrow within him. The words were good to hear, and he hadn't known how desperately he'd needed to hear them.

"Thank you," he said softly, releasing her hands. Candice ambled back to Jack once again, taking his hand in hers. "Is the baby doing okay?" Brad asked, his voice hoarse with emotion.

Candice beamed. He remembered a time when he'd found her the most attractive girl in Bethel.

"Yes." Her cheeks pinked with gladness. "It's a boy," she said.

A boy. Brad's heart stuttered over itself. A son. There would be a little boy with his features born any day now, gauging by the wide spread of Candice's stomach.

"Are you going to keep him?" The paperwork he'd signed hadn't been clear.

Smiling, Candice shook her head. "No, I've decided to place him for adoption to a good family."

A previously unfelt pain pulsed in his chest at her words. It was sadness mixed with relief. He wouldn't make a good father of this he was sure, and Candice was still so young. They both were. "The family he's going to—are they good people?"

Candice and Jack nodded at the same time, but it was Jack who spoke. "The Andersons are wonderful people. Godly, church-going folk. Everyone who knows them says they will be great parents to the little guy."

A moment of jealousy came at the easy way Jack referred to the baby. But then again, he had the right to, and Brad didn't. Jack had been there for Candice in a way that Brad hadn't. He pushed down the emotion. He should be happy for her—and he was. Still . . .

"I'm glad," he said. Brad slid his hands into his pockets, wishing— not for the first time—that Amy was here. If she was, though, this would probably be even more awkward. He suddenly wished he and Candice were alone; but it didn't look like Jack would be too receptive to that, and Brad didn't blame him.

"How have you been?" It seemed like a strange question to ask as it came out of his mouth, but he thought Candice would understand.

After all, there was a time when they had known each other quite well. She'd been the one who had held him when he'd had another fight with his father. She understood how much he missed his mother.

Candice ran her hand down her baby bump, and she looked so peaceful. He envied that. What had she found that made her look like that?

"I'm fine." She smiled up at Jack. "Life is good."

She was happy, and he was glad for her happiness. He wasn't in love with Candice. But they had shared something special—and he knew that he would always be a part of her, as she would forever be a part of him.

He deliberately looked Jack and Candice both in the eyes before saying, "I am happy for you both, and I can see that you are happy, too."

He turned his gaze to Candice again. "You'll let me know when he's born?" he asked. His father had made him sign off his parental rights, and at the time, he'd believed it was the right thing to do. However, a part of him, which was steadily getting bigger by the day, desperately wanted to know what would happen to his son, even if he could not be a part of his life.

Candice's eyes widened in surprise, and then that familiar smile he'd always loved lifted her mouth. "Of course, Brad, we will let you know. D-do you want to come to the birth?"

Did he? No, Jack was the man for that job. He shook his head and returned her smile tentatively. "No, I would just like to know when he is born."

There was no condemnation in Candice's gaze as he met it again. "Okay."

His time in Westwood was drawing to a close; he had fulfilled his reason for coming. Brad held out his hand to Jack, and when Jack reached out and shook it, he said, "Thank you, Jack."

The other man nodded. "It was my pleasure." Brad didn't doubt for a second that it was.

"I guess I'll see you around," he said.

"It was good to see you, Brad," Candice said, reaching for his hand and squeezing it gently before letting go.

"Goodbye."

"Bye."

Thirty minutes later, his tires were eating up the road between Westwood and Bethel. He had some other bridges to fix and far more peace to make before his journey was over.

CHAPTER TWENTY-EIGHT

All was quiet when Brad eventually returned to the dark, imposing structure that was his home. Danika's new silver Mercedes stood beside his father's new Audi R8. His father had always had a distinguished taste in cars, but since Danika had joined in the picture, his taste had become more extravagant. Brad knew the cost of the cars, and the thought made him shudder.

He shouldn't worry about the way his father was lavishly spending his money on his new bride; it was expected to be that way, right? He didn't know Danika well enough to know if she was a gold-digger, and his father, however blind as he could be, was an astute judge of character—or he had been; Brad hoped that he still was. Danika *seemed* sincere.

The door of his truck clattered closed in the near-silent night, and he thanked Ira for driving. He glanced down at his phone and checked the time. It was a little after midnight. A lonely light illuminated the front of the house, and through the windows, he could see a few lights on. Danika and his father must have already retired for the night. Or they were out at another dinner party or fundraiser and would be dragging themselves into bed in a few hours, courtesy of Ira. It didn't matter; he needed the time to himself, anyway.

He stretched and yawned as he turned the key in the lock of the front door and let himself in. He was tired. They'd driven straight from Westwood, five hours straight, stopping only for gas. He had been eager to get back home. But it was more than just fatigue; his mind was tired. He had spent the entire drive back from Bethel thinking about Candice and the baby, about Griffin and the emails they'd exchanged since Brad had left Heavenly Haven, and—of course—about Amy.

Amy. His gut tightened, and his jaw tensed. There was so much he needed to say to her, so much for which he needed to apologize. She had said that until he forgave himself and let go of his crutch, there was no place for peace and healing. She hadn't been wrong, and he knew that now—if only it hadn't taken him so long to figure it out.

Her bright blue eyes, red-rimmed and wet with tears, flittered through his memory. He should have known she would never betray him. She did it because she cared about him and wanted him to be free. He'd been so stupid to believe otherwise, but anger was rarely a rational animal. He should have known that taking a step down the pathway with Hank would lead to trouble, and it had. Amy had been there to clean up his mess, but he should have done it himself.

He felt a sad smile lift his mouth as he remembered the kiss they'd shared at Jace's party. He wondered again why she'd run away and then friend-zoned him. Was it because she cared about him as more than a friend? Or was it because, at the time, he was on a path that would only lead to destruction? He would never know unless he asked her. But would he be brave enough to do that?

Brad was ready to clean up his life. Amy didn't know that yet, and he hadn't been sure of it himself until recently. He missed being with her. Like an ache inside him that wouldn't pass, he wanted to be with her, but her final words still lingered in his heart. Candice was in the past; she'd granted her forgiveness, and his own journey of forgiveness was on its way. But there was still more forgiveness to be sought.

Exhausted from his journey, he walked quickly up the long, wooden staircase gleaming dully in the entryway. He crossed the second-floor threshold and walked to his father's room, peering inside. Near darkness greeted his eyes, but he could see that the bed was made. His father and Danika must be out for the evening.

Relieved, he crossed to his room and flopped down on his bed, staring at the dark ceiling before flipping on the bedside lamp. The Bible Griffin had given him on his first night at Heavenly Haven sat where he'd thrown it on his bedside table the day he'd returned home in a fit of anger. He sat up, lifted the thick book from the table, and flipped through the pages, remembering verses he'd heard in Bible class—and some, he remembered from his conversations with Griffin.

"Be strong and courageous. Do not be afraid or terrified because of them, for the Lord your God goes with you; he will never leave you nor forsake you" (Deut. 31:6).

"Come to me, all you who are weary and burdened, and I will give you rest" (Matt. 11:28).

"For God so loved the world that he gave his one and only Son, that whoever believes in him shall not perish but have eternal life" (John 3:16).

As he sat there, more and more verses came to him, until the weight of his thoughts pressed into him like a shroud. He'd thought the weight would be gone after he'd spoken with Candice, but Amy had been right. The only way he would find peace and healing was to forgive himself and to allow God to forgive him of his terrible and thoughtless mistakes.

Brad buried his face in his hands and prayed the words he knew by heart but had never made his own. Forgiveness, like a tender hand, swept through the remaining mounds of mud; and at last, his soul was clean. The guilt from his betrayal and rejection of Candice was washed away by the love of His Savior. Tears ran down his cheeks—more than he had ever let fall.

He grabbed blindly at a pillow behind him and wept the tears he'd tried to keep hidden from the day his mother had died, leaving him with a man who knew only the love language of money. Waves of sadness ebbed and flowed as he wordlessly poured out his sorrow, his guilt, and his pain. He was forgiven. The heavy weight that had clouded his every thought and judgment from the time he'd walked away from her was gone, lifted and taken, never to return. He was finally free.

Brad pulled himself up and flipped on the main light, awakening the ensuite bathroom light. A shower sounded like a great idea—and then he'd find some food.

When the bathroom was misted up and his shower done, he quickly dressed and made his way down to the kitchen. Mrs. McCleary had left a dinner for him—bless her heart. He pulled it out and heated it up. Setting the plate of chicken pot pie, fresh beans, and roasted potatoes on the dining room table, he dug in, remembering all the meals he'd shared with Amy and the others at Heavenly Haven.

Amy was his next order of business. How would he convince her that he had changed? That she didn't need to worry about him hurting himself anymore? That he'd finally found the forgiveness he'd been desperately seeking, and it was so much better than the numbness he'd found at the bottom of a bottle? He didn't even know if she was back home yet. He would have to find out.

When the meal was done, he did something he never did: wash his dishes. Mrs. McCleary would probably have a coronary if she saw him; she had always prided herself on doing her job to the highest quality, and that included never allowing either of the Thorn men to do anything on his own.

He chuckled as he thought of her face when she saw the dishes. Chuckling still, he brushed his teeth and slipped under the covers of his bed once again. He dragged his laptop nearer and began to type.

> *Griffin,*
>
> *You wouldn't believe what happened today. But before I get to that, I want to say thank you for not giving up on me, and thank you for taking the time to check in and help me, even if it isn't your job. I can't tell you how much I appreciate it.*
>
> *I went to Westwood today to speak to Candice, and you know, you were right. She had already forgiven me for being such a . . . well, you get the picture . . .*

His eyes grew heavier and heavier as the emotional expenditure slowly caught up with his weary body. He would need to finish the email tomorrow. He set the laptop on the floor beside him and soon welcomed the arms of sleep.

Today was a day to celebrate. She was going home. Amy's grip tightened on the zipper of her duffle bag as she scanned her room at Heavenly Haven. Everything was in its place, just the way she'd found it when she had arrived a month ago. Despite all that had happened in the last four weeks, she was grateful to have spent them at Heavenly Haven.

Her heart panged again as she thought of Brad. She truly hoped he'd found peace. She'd tried to help him, but in the end, she should have known that she couldn't heal him—only God could do that. Just like Jesus was the One Who could help her move past the hurts of yesterdays and look forward to her tomorrows. There would still be many circumstances to handle—like her parents and their confusing relationship, returning to school, finishing her senior year, and seeing Brad. She hoped she would see him again next week at school.

"Amy, it's time to go," Mildred said, peeking her head around the corner into Amy's room. "Barely looks like anyone lived here," she said. "Thank you for being so thorough. You have saved me hours of work."

Pleasure spilled onto Amy's cheeks. "No, thank *you*, Mildred. You've . . . " She swallowed back the tears and cleared her throat. "Thank you for helping me. I don't know how I can possibly say it enough."

"A simple thank you and the joy I see shining in your eyes are thanks enough for this old woman." Mildred wrapped her arms around Amy and hugged her. Amy sank into the embrace, joy flowing from her eyes and into the linen fabric at Mildred's shoulder.

Mildred stepped back and wiped a lone tear from Amy's cheek. "Remember all you have heard and learned and take the journey one step at a time. It might take a lifetime, but with God, healing is possible."

"I know." She knew that her journey was not over—in fact, this part of her journey to healing was coming to an end, but a whole new one would start once she was home.

"Do you have the number for the counselor in Bethel?"

Amy nodded. "Here in my pocket," she said, patting the front of her jeans.

"And your Bible?"

"In my bag."

"I guess you're ready to go. Oh, before I forget!" Mildred hurried out of the room and, in a flash, reappeared holding a wrapped package. "Griffin asked me if you could give this to Brad. I don't know if you're going to see him. He thought, seeing as you both live in the same town and go to the same school, maybe you could pass it on."

Amy swallowed back her tears. "I will try to drop it off at his dad's house. I don't know if I'm going to see Brad anytime soon, but the least I can do is put this in the mailbox."

"Griffin would be most grateful. Okay, well, if that is everything, let's get you checked out and onto the road. Your brother is waiting in the lobby for you."

"Thank you, Mildred—for everything."

"You are most welcome."

Mildred hurried from the room, presumably to a waiting Logan. Amy placed the red package in her bag.

Her time at Heavenly Haven was over. She was going home.

CHAPTER TWENTY-NINE

Why was he staring at her? Brad's penetrating gaze burned into her. She felt the weight of it as she bent her head closer to Felicia's in an effort to hear what her friend was saying.

"Sorry, what?" Amy asked.

Felicia glanced down the hallway, smiling at Brad as she beckoned him closer. "I said, it's so good to see you at school again. I mean, I was worried I was going to have to graduate all by myself."

Amy laughed and curled her arm around her friend's neck. "I wouldn't do that to you! Besides, I'm just as glad to be back." The laughter died in her throat as Brad sauntered up to them. There was something different about him, about the way his eyes held hers and his smile spread across his face. What was it?

"Hey, Felicia. Amy."

It was in the way he said her name, too. Maybe she was imagining it, but his voice was so gentle and kind as he said her name—like it was important to him.

Again, the guilt of the missed calls and messages curled in her stomach. He'd even spoken with her mother and her father—and Logan, when he'd been home for the weekend. But she'd never called back. She'd wanted to. She'd considered giving into her mother's pleading to put Brad out of his misery—but something had held her back.

It wasn't a question of forgiving him for the way they'd parted at Heavenly Haven; she knew now that both of them needed the time away from each other to grow and heal. Well, *she* had, at least—she wasn't sure about Brad. But as she gazed into those gentle blue eyes that seemed so focused on her, she wondered again.

"Hey, Brad, I was just telling Amy how grateful I am to have you guys back at school. Now, I don't need to make that long trip across the stage at graduation alone. You know what I mean?"

Brad nodded, but he didn't look at Felicia, His gaze was fixed on her—with toe-curling intensity. "Yeah, it's great to be back." He raised his eyebrow in a silent question. Was he waiting for her to say the same or something?

"Ah, yeah, good to be back." Goodness—when did she lose her senses? Or was it because for the first time in what felt like months, she was talking to the person she thought of nonstop? Felicia glanced between the two of them, her eyebrow raised. She caught Amy's gaze.

"I think I see Jace over there waiting for me, so . . . " Felicia darted away, and then they were alone—or as alone as two people could be in a bustling hallway.

"You didn't answer any of my texts," Brad said. A hint of hurt lingered in his voice. "Why?"

The answer would leave her vulnerable. "I wasn't ready," she said, finally. It was the truth—but only half of it. She wasn't ready to let herself hope. Maybe she was now.

Brad's brow tipped in confusion. "I get that, but . . . " The warning bell rang, taking away his chance to explain. Before heading to first period, Brad reached out, stopping her from turning. "Can we talk at lunch?" he asked.

"I have a meeting with Mr. Rory about graduation," she said, putting some distance between them.

"Okay, what about going for coffee? Second Cup, after school?"

Amy paused and drew a deep breath. "Okay. Now, we better get going."

Together, they entered science class, each weaving to their separate desks. It felt so weird being back in the classroom. Amy could feel the eyes of her classmates on her, silently wondering where she'd been for the last month. Or maybe she was just overthinking it, like she usually did.

She needed to relax. Yes, some of her classmates must be wondering—and if they were brave enough to ask, she would probably tell them the truth—but it wasn't any of their business where she'd been or why.

Taking a few deep breaths and mentally preparing herself for the lesson, she took out her final assignment. She'd missed the deadline; however, Principal Rory and Mrs. Wilson had met with her mother and father and given her permission to hand in any overdue work as soon as possible. She stood from her desk, purposely ignoring the questioning gazes that followed her.

"I have my assignment, Mrs. Wilson."

Mrs. Wilson stopped shuffling the stack of papers on her desk and lifted her gaze to Amy.

"Amy, it's lovely to have you back. How are you?"

Her cheeks heated. "I'm doing much better. Thank you for giving me extra time to do the assignment."

She put the papers in Mrs. Wilson's waiting hand and returned to her seat. Anxiety swirled in her gut as she watched her teacher study them. And then a bright smile eclipsed the older woman's face. She glanced at Amy and nodded once, beaming. Happiness drowned her anxiety. *Thank You, Jesus.*

The rest of the school day went similarly, except for one glaring difference—instead of hanging with the other football players, Brad seemed to be playing her shadow. At lunch, after her meeting with the principal, she'd found him pacing the floor outside the office, waiting for her. And he didn't even say why, but he'd walked her to the cafeteria. It was weird. She felt her cheeks heat each time Felicia met her gaze and waggled her eyebrows. Brad seemed to be oblivious, although she did catch him staring longingly at her more than once. Why was he being so weird?

At last, Amy heard the final bell. After sending a quick text to her mother, she drove to Second Cup. Brad had made it there before her, and she briefly wondered how before acknowledging that he *did* drive like a lunatic sometimes.

She pushed open the door, and a bell tingled, announcing her entrance. Brad sat at the back of the room in a blue booth. He hadn't noticed her yet, but she could see his leg bouncing on the tips of his toes as he waited for her, his fingers drumming an unconscious beat atop the white table. When he did see her, the most breathtaking smile lit up his face, and she felt her heart pound in response.

"You came," he said, standing from his seat and gently guiding her back to the booth.

"I said I would."

"I know, but I wasn't sure because, you know . . . " Brad trailed off, waiting for her to take her seat before taking his. He sat facing her, and an awkward silence descended. There was so much to talk about, but they couldn't seem to bring themselves to say anything.

Drawing a deep breath, Amy laid her hands flat on the tabletop. Brad swallowed, glanced at her, and then took her hands between his. That beautiful smile reappeared.

"How have you been?" he asked softly, smoothing his fingers over hers.

"I, ah . . . I've been good. I mean, fine." She cleared her throat. "And you?"

Brad studied her again. "Much better . . ." He sighed, then seemed to be lost in his exploration of her hand.

The waitress came and took their orders. A cappuccino for Brad and a chai latte for herself. When the drinks arrived, they sipped them in companionable silence, although Brad did not let go of her hand.

"Brad," she said after a while, "why did you ask me to come?"

He swallowed hard. "I owe you an apology," he said. "And I wanted to thank you."

"Thank me?"

"Yes, I want to thank you for telling me off."

What?

"Amy, what happened at the campout made me think. I was mad, but a lot has happened since then. Anyway, I'm sorry."

"It's all right, Brad. I understand; I really do." And she did. What happened that last day at Heavenly Haven had hurt, but it had made her realize two things: that she wasn't ready to be involved with anyone and that her caring for Brad had gone way beyond the barriers of friendship. She didn't love him yet; but it would not take much, and she acknowledged that.

"Still, I'm sorry for the way I left things that day with you at Heavenly Haven. I understand why you told Griffin, and honestly, I'm thankful for it now. Without that wake-up call, I never would have taken the steps necessary to clean up my life."

Amy choked on a sip of tea and hacked until it cleared. "That's just the thing, Brad. Why won't you believe me? I never said anything to Griffin."

Brad's jaw went slack, and then he slowly nodded. "I'm sorry," he whispered. "You have been a great friend to me, Amy. I hope we stay friends, even if we have a lot to sort out."

Her heart pinged painfully in her chest. She'd been wrong. The kiss that they had shared at Jace's had been a spur-of-the-moment thing, and it didn't mean anything more to Brad than that. "Of course, we can be friends."

Instead of happiness, Brad's face crumpled with disappointment. He sighed heavily. "I'm glad."

The same emotion that beat in her chest was reflected in his eyes. Was there something more between them, after all? In the months past, she'd learned a lot about being brave, being assertive, and taking the time to let people know how she felt. She drew on that bravery.

"What is it, Brad?" she asked. At Heavenly Haven, they'd been so honest with each other. They'd held each other up, and she'd hoped their relationship was back on stable grounds.

Brad swallowed hard again. He set his coffee on the other side of the table. Then, to her surprise, he took the cup from her hand and placed it beside his before taking both her hands. His sapphire eyes were soft and open. Oh . . .

"I want to be more than friends with you, Amy Carter. I'm crazy about you," Brad said softly. Tenderly, he ran his fingers over hers, looking at her like she was the first brave bud after a long winter's night.

She was wrong—the kiss *had* meant something to him, too. Heat filled her cheeks as she remembered his lips pressed sweetly to hers.

"And I wondered if perhaps you felt the same about me?" His Adam's apple bobbed up and down as he swallowed, holding her gaze. She, too, was unable to look away. Her heart beat faster, little sparks of happiness dancing in her stomach like fairies.

"Yes," she said softly, the heat in her cheeks growing in intensity. "I'm crazy about you, too."

In the next instant, Brad let go of her hands and shuffled along the booth until he was right beside her. Tentatively, his arms enfolded her into his chest, while with one hand, he lifted her chin. "I'm going to kiss you now," he whispered. He leaned in closer, his lips brushing hers. This kiss was better than the kiss they'd shared at the party—so much better.

ACKNOWLEDGMENTS

Writing a book is like producing a piece of art. Each piece of the story reveals the full picture of the author's presentation. The *Bethel Private School Series* has provided me with the opportunity to create awareness through fiction for our young people today.

In this, I would like to thank Anna Riebe Raats and Katie Smith for their continued support and hard work in the process of releasing these stories out into a world that is in such desperate need of the love of Christ.

I want to thank my family for bearing with the countless hours it takes to write, edit, and finalize these stories.

Thank you to my friends Val Witter and Sharon Bulmer, whose prayers have been with me and my family.

What would we do without the love of Christ? To my Savior and King, thank You for Your precious sacrifice for me.

NEXT IN THE BETHEL PRIVATE SCHOOL SERIES . . .
IT'S YOU, AGAIN . . .

CHAPTER ONE

"You have got to be kidding me." Felicia Wren gaped at the tall, broad-shouldered man before her, his muscular arms akimbo on his narrow cargo short covered hips. He stared wordlessly back at her, his own expression mirrored the shock she was sure was on her face. A line from the movie *Casablanca* whispered in her memory, "Of all the gin joints in all the towns, in all the world, she walks into mine." In this case it was a *he* and they were at the airport. But, still, the irony was the same.

"Fe?" His arms dropped to his sides. "What are you doing here?" Confusion momentarily forgotten, he opened his arms and stepped forward to embrace her. Felicia recovered herself enough to lift her arms and stop him from wrapping those sky blue t-shirt-covered really nice arms around her shoulders and drawing her into a hug. Her and Trent Anson didn't hug anymore. In fact, they didn't anything anymore. They weren't best friends, they weren't boyfriend and girlfriend. They were nothing. And it was all Trent's fault. She should walk away. The angry beat of her blood through her veins was telling her to. She didn't. Maybe it was nostalgia, maybe it was the fact that instead of taking a trip to see her Aunt Aida in Hawaii with her friends, Willow Rysen, Candice Hillman, and Amy Carter, she was making the trip alone. Maybe that was the reason she gave herself for not turning on her heel and ignoring him the way she had all the times he'd come with an apology.

"I could ask you the same thing," she said. She lifted her faux tan leather carry-on messenger bag higher onto her shoulder, gripping the strap tightly between her suddenly shaking hands. Her yellow tank rode slightly up from her waistline, and she smoothed it with a flurry of her hands over the waistband of her light blue capri jeans. Her thin orange cardigan fluttered to the floor, and she dipped down to retrieve it before straightening again. Who knew what had been on the floor with all these people here. The airport around them buzzed with life and Trent seemed to find something she did amusing. The constant hum of voices, announcements, baggage trolleys, and the smack of plastic wheels over smooth tiles rang in the early morning air of the terminal. The beginning of the summer holidays always brought extra traffic to Fort MacMurray International Airport. And this summer was no different.

"Summer holiday with Michael and the gang." He shrugged as if there was no bad blood between the two of them. Like they were friends who had just met at an airport and were having a pleasant conversation. Two years ago they would have been, but not anymore. Trent looked the same, just as handsome as he had when her feelings for him had gone from the friendzone to something more. His sun-bleached dirty blond hair was exactly the same shade as she remembered. Those light blue eyes so much like her own looked at her in a way that made her feel seen. He had always had that effect on her. Back then it was endearing to her, but after Willow, it was something that she detested. He had known how she felt and yet he had done it anyway. She pushed the painful memory away. It was water under the bridge as the saying went. It's a pity water didn't wash away betrayal as easily as dirt. *Think of something else Felicia,* she commanded herself.

"That's nice," she said noncommittally.

An awkward silence descended between them as they joined the check-in line. She remembered a time when they never ran out of things to say to each other, but that was in the past. And if she had anything to do about it, it would stay that way.

For more information about
Michelle Dykman
and
You Found Me
please visit:

www.michelledykman.com

For more information about
AMBASSADOR INTERNATIONAL
please visit:

www.ambassador-international.com

Thank you for reading this book. Please consider leaving us a review on your favorite retailer's website, Goodreads or Bookbub, or our website.

Abandoned as infants, Tovi and her twin brother were raised by an eclectic tribe of warm, kind people in a treehouse village in the valley. After her brother's sudden disappearance Tovi questions her life and her faith in an invisible King. Ignoring her best friend Silas' advice, she decides to search for her brother in the kingdom on top of the mountain. Amidst the glamour of the kingdom above the cloud Tovi is torn between her own dark desires and unanswered questions.

When Ari finds herself with a job offer to work undercover and find her purpose again, she can't resist. But as her undercover case deepens, she discovers that the voices in her head aren't as imaginary as she thought.

After department layoffs and an increase in crime, Crime Scene Specialist and Bloodstain Pattern Analyst Renee' McKenzie develops her own crime scene team of junior interns, including her own daughter, Bailey. The team arrives to their biggest crime scene yet, and Bailey's father, DEA Agent Liam McKenzie, is brought in to help with the investigation as the "players" of this case appear to be connected to something bigger than a local narcotics investigation.